MW00945517

BREAKING
BACKBONES
INFORMATION IS POWER

To Daniel
and Jos. Mahalo
for your encouragement
with Alohas
Dekel (myhacker
handle)

"Deb Radcliff knows how to craft a riveting cyber-spy thriller that reads like a high-speed car chase through the intersection of the real world and cyberspace. Backed by Deb's years of experience as an investigative journalist covering cybersecurity, Breaking Backbones is an up-all-night page-turner told by an insider."

—Diana Kelley, formerly cybersecurity CTO at Microsoft and co-founder of the Security Curve analyst firm.

"Deb Radcliff weaves real world cyberattack methodology into a gripping tale. I did not want to put this one down as the characters and plot came alive. Can't wait till the next installment comes out."

—Stephen Northcutt, founder, GIAC cybersecurity certification series, founding president, SANS Technology Institute, graduate school.

—BOOK I OF THE HACKER TRILOGY—

BREAKING BACKBONES

INFORMATION IS POWER

DEB RADCLIFF

ARCHWAY
PUBLISHING

Archway Publishing books may be ordered through booksellers or by contacting:

Archway Publishing
1663 Liberty Drive
Bloomington, IN 47403
www.archwaypublishing.com
844-669-3957

Because of the dynamic nature of the Internet, any web addresses or
links contained in this book may have changed since publication and
may no longer be valid. The views expressed in this work are solely those
of the author and do not necessarily reflect the views of the publisher,
and the publisher hereby disclaims any responsibility for them.

Any people depicted in stock imagery provided by Getty Images are
models, and such images are being used for illustrative purposes only.
Certain stock imagery © Getty Images.

ISBN: 978-1-6657-0108-2 (sc)
ISBN: 978-1-6657-0109-9 (hc)
ISBN: 978-1-6657-0110-5 (e)

Library of Congress Control Number: 2021906661

Print information available on the last page.

Archway Publishing rev. date: 06/02/2021

Wikipedia: A **backbone** ... is a part of computer network that interconnects various pieces of network ... A backbone can tie together diverse networks in the same building, in different buildings in a campus environment, or over wide areas. Normally, the *backbone's capacity is greater than the networks connected to it.* (emphasis added)

CHAPTER 1.

OPERATION BACKBONE

The sound of gunfire spurs her on as Cy programs furiously into her wrist device. She is crouched behind a cinder block enclosure normally used for GlobeCom waste recycle. Bullets ricochet off the cinder block walls in little puffs of dust all around her. All the while, a drone war plays out above.

As Cy prepares to execute her code, her fighters are throwing everything they've got at the GlobeCom drones—modified semiautomatics, hot lasers, drone signal scramblers, and their own home-built fighting drones, which are woefully outnumbered.

This is Operation Backbone, a hacker war seventeen years in the making.

Information is power, as the hackers say. In a system ripe for abuse, GlobeCom has taken over most of the world's data and now controls the global population through human chip implants called unique identifiers, or UIs. At this moment, dozens of hacker strike teams around the world are attempting to relieve GlobeCom of its iron grip on humanity through a global, coordinated attack.

It's five in the morning, nearly dawn at the Oakridge hub where Cy is flanked by her fellow hacker freedom fighters who duck and fire from behind the waste bins. This campus houses the largest computational system in the United States and was primary headquarters for the former US National Reconnaissance Office before GlobeCom took control. Now it's one of dozens of GlobeCom data centers around the world.

The hacker team members wear copper mesh masks to scramble GlobeCom's facial scanners. The mask is making Cy feel overheated and a little light-headed.

"You said the window is two minutes, right?" Cy shouts to her wingman on the left named Des (short for Des0l8tion).

Des taps her once—for yes—on her shoulder.

Beside Cy and to her right, Allure is directing their action through her Visual Aid Goggles. She is also feeling the heat. She raises her face gear for just a second to catch her breath.

"My VAGs are fogging," Allure says, fanning her face with her hand before dropping the mask and VAGs down again.

Wiry and quick, Allure stands six feet tall without shoes and weighs a scant 130 pounds. She is dressed in battle fatigues with her flack vest cinched tight like a corset, emphasizing her long, lean shape.

In another garbage enclosure across a narrow drive from them, Cy's two other team members, Skew and Elven (father and son), are hacking GlobeCom control signals to drop the GlobeCom attack drones from the sky and mess with the automated guns firing from rooftop turrets around them.

From his side of the enclosure, Des nods for Elven, who then switches interfaces to take control of Des's fighting drones so Des can focus on the suicide birds.

"Starting countdown," Des shouts above the din so Cy can hear him.

Des reaches his muscled left arm over Cy's right shoulder, resting it there familiarly. Steering his drones with his right hand, he raises his fingers on his left hand so Cy can see him counting.

"... three, two, one."

The suicide drones slam the wall in formation and explode with a deafening boom. Cy can't look just now, but she swears Des must be smiling, given how much he loves blowing things up.

The explosion clears a ten-foot hole through the back wall to the data center. As the dust settles, they see the GlobeCom's skeleton crew members scrambling out through the interior door to the lobby to get away from the destruction. Allure, still directing through her VAGs, watches the last person exit before the door automatically locks behind him.

With the reinforced wall out of the way, Cy's malware hijacks the emergency communications network through a proximity attack, shuts it down, and hops into GlobeCom's building and security controls. From there, the malware turns off the temperature controls and fire-suppression systems before spreading to thousands of multiprocessing and quantum computing systems racked floor-to-ceiling in a cooled, warehouse-sized server room.

As Cy's code executes, Allure monitors the heat signatures in the data center.

"Wait. Wait! Someone's still in there moving around," Allure yells.

"Shit!" Cy responds. "There's no time for this."

Allure executes another command, and then the door unlocks and opens. She adds, "OK, OK, I've got it."

The trapped data analyst, a young Asian woman, races out through the door, which shuts and locks behind her.

"So, you sure there's nobody else in there we don't know about?" Cy asks.

"No, there's no one else. The only heat signatures I'm picking up are the overheating servers," Allure responds.

As the malware spreads across the systems, a military-grade wipe-and-destroy program erases and shreds the data and the operating programs. It then reaches down to the hardware, causing the electronics to pop and catch fire. For good measure, the malware also follows the data pathway to off-site backup systems, where it repeats the same process.

"Done!" Cy shouts, lifting her mask so she can breathe.

The sky is dawning, and Des looks up worriedly at more incoming GlobeCom drones. "We've got to get a move on!" he says.

As they pull back, Allure, who's as tall as Des without her heels on, raises a fist in defiance and shouts the hacker creed. "Information is *power*! Information should be *free*!"

The five of them run through the back lot toward their escape vehicle waiting at the edge of the forest. Ahead of them, Elven and Skew steer their remaining drones through an open rear door and into the large Faraday bins waiting in the back of their vintage, tricked-out Humvee. Because it lacks any so-called smart digital features that produce signals, the car is mostly undetectable by GlobeCom scanners.

Mane, a large fellow with shoulder-length, auburn plated hair that makes him look like a lion, is in the driver's seat ready to start the engine. He monitors four GlobeCom drones bearing down on them with weapons engaged.

"Hurry! Hurry!" shouts Mane, a slight Bronx accent to his voice. "Manned vehicles just around the corner."

The team hears the sound of tires screeching, and they hustle even faster to get their gear off and into the vehicle.

"Off them and drop them!" Mane orders.

At this point, everyone powers off their electronics and seals them in Faraday bags before tossing the bags into the drone bins, which are also Faraday-lined.

Skew and Elven seal the bins to protect their devices from the EMP as Allure jumps onboard behind the passenger seat. She pulls out the EMP (electro-magnetic pulse) gun, which looks like a small radio dish with a gun-like handle, and points it at the drones and vehicles bearing down on them.

"Initiating EMP," she cautions.

Allure fires. The pulse drops the drones to the ground, their useless weapons dangling and broken. Having just come around the corner, GlobeCom's silver, tubular-shaped security vehicles also fail and slow to a stop, as do all their weapons and communication systems.

Cy is making a beeline for the open side door Allure just fired from, with Des in-line right behind her.

"Safe!" Cy shouts as she heaves herself inside the vehicle.

Just then, something fast and powerful slams her in the lower back, throwing her face-first onto the Humvee floor. In the same moment, Des grunts from behind and lands on top of her, deadweight.

Blood puddles on the floor between them. It's hard to tell whose it is.

CHAPTER 2.

AFTERMATH

From far away and through a tunnel, Cy hears Allure screaming, her normally sultry voice now high-pitched and nasally.

"Shit! Shit! Shit! Shit! Shit! *Shiiit!*"

Allure fires another pulse at the lone GlobeCom drone, dropping it to the ground. She then helps Elven tug Des off of Cy, while Mane unwraps the starter and fires up the engine.

Cy hears voices and doors slamming and peeling tires. But she can't move—can't speak—can hardly breathe. Wait. Is she breathing? She doesn't know.

Allure removes her mask first to reveal a long, oval face with intense dark eyes and long black lashes. Then she kneels beside Cy and Des and takes off Cy's mask next. Cy, an earthy-looking woman in her midforties has a heart-shaped face and dark hair with fine white strands like salt on pepper. She looks pale and lifeless, except for her jagged breathing.

"Cy? Cy! Don't you die on me," cries Allure. "Can you hear me, girl? I said *don't die!*"

Mane shifts the gear to off-road turbo, and they disappear into the forest.

Allure gently turns Cy on her side, looking for a wound. Then she pushes up Cy's flak vest to see a dark red stain in the middle of Cy's back.

"Get me a body board!" she orders.

Elven and Skew, who are removing their drones from the Faraday bins to send out again as lookouts, respond immediately.

Skew is fully Irish, middle-aged, and pot-bellied with long red hair and a gray-streaked beard. Elven, twenty-two, is small and fit. He has his mother's black skin and wiry orange hair from his father. Elven keeps the crazy hair under control with a short butch cut.

Skew and Elven wrench a bodyboard from under the rear seats and pass it over to Allure. As he looks at Des and Cy on the floor of the Humvee, Elven feels faint.

"Oh, man there's so, so much blood," Elven says with worry. "Da? Are they going to be OK? Da?"

Skew, who's as shaken as Elven, tries to put on a brave face for his son.

"I—I don't know, Son. I don't know," Skew answers honestly. "But they're both breathing. That's a good sign."

Once she's secured Cy on the bodyboard, Allure reaches over to remove Des's mask. When she does, they collectively gasp.

"It must be bad from the sounds you all are making back there," Mane observes from the front seat.

Des is on his side, his hazel eyes open but dazed. He's lightly gurgling and pressing on his neck in a vain attempt to stop a flow of blood that's passing through his fingers and pooling like a halo beneath his head.

Even in this state, Des is fierce and beautiful. At forty-seven, he still looks like a Ken doll, military style—chiseled with short-cropped, sandy-blond hair and only a few light sunlines around the eyes and mouth.

Allure tries to apply more pressure to Des's neck, looking at him and then back at Cy as she puts it together.

"Oh my God," she says with irony. "I ... I think the fucking GlobeCom drone got the *both of them* ... with a *single shot!*"

TWENTY YEARS EARLIER

Cy used to be Cindy Frank, a hotshot digital forensics expert for the Department of Defense (DoD).

At seventeen, before she got kicked out of the foster system, she followed her passion and enrolled as a charity case for the NSA's Center of Excellence Program to earn her master's in Information Security at Syracuse University. She took the accelerated program, and by the age of twenty, she was recruited to the Department of Defense Computer Forensics Labs (DFL), which picked up her college bills in exchange for a two-year work commitment. She stayed longer than that and never planned to leave, despite that government contracting paid half of what she could earn in the private sector.

Cindy felt at home surrounded by the dim blue lights and blinking monitors that made up her workspace. She loved how the DFL had a true crime lab for cyber—from the evidence locker to the super-cooled, two-thousand-square-foot server room housing the multiquantum processors that sifted petabytes of digital evidence.

All this magic hidden in a four-floor, nondescript business building in Linthicum, about thirty miles outside of Bethesda.

After four years into the job, her world was about to change forever …

"Come upstairs, Cindy. I have someone here for you to meet," said Cindy's director, Col. Chris James, US Army.

He was speaking to her through a video chat window on her computer. Closing in on age seventy but with no sign of retiring, Colonel James's dark brown hair was whitening and thinning against his skin, which was pink and weathered from the time he spent on his sailboat.

"Yes, sir. Be right up," said Cindy.

As she rose, she directed the chat to her video goggles and continued the conversation while walking down the hallway toward the elevator. She was trying to see into his office but could only catch the bookshelf (overstuffed) and whiteboard (blank) behind him.

"May I ask what this is about, sir?" she asked.

"We'll talk when you get into the office," he said before disconnecting.

While not enlisted herself, Cindy, a contractor for the DoD, knew the chain of command and respected it for what it was. With Colonel James as her mentor, she had nothing to fear from the rest of the brass, so long as she continued to learn, perform, and improve the investigative standards and forensically sound outcomes of her cases.

At the end of the fourth-floor hallway in front of Colonel James's office, she paused to look out a bank of windows and collect her thoughts. The freezing wind was blowing the falling snow sideways in the empty front lot facing Elkridge Landing Road.

"Another deathly cold day in Linthicum," she said to herself.

Fresh tire tracks in the snow indicated that two vehicles had just driven down to the underground garage. After four years working here, she never did learn what the above-ground front lot was used for. It was always empty. Everyone parked underground, including the visitors.

Cindy turned from the window, opened the door that said "Director," and stepped into the colonel's old-style mahogany-paneled corner office. She straightened and raised her arm to solute.

"Cindy, no need. You're a civilian," said Colonel James.

She dropped her arm, and James stood up along with a tall, distinguished-looking four-star general, dark black skin, about fifty years old. As they waited for her to take her seat, their actions reminded her of how very polite enlisted people were.

The younger man still sitting turned toward her and flashed a brilliant white smile. He looked like a young Brad Pitt with wide cheeks, steel gray eyes, and fine wire-rimmed glasses.

"I'd stand too, but I'm a little tied down at the moment," he said, nodding toward his left wrist, which was handcuffed to his chair.

Cindy raised an eyebrow then turned to Colonel James with a questioning look.

"This is someone who wanted to meet you, Cindy," James explained.

The man seated in front of her was far too well dressed to be military or government. And much too brash …

"Nice to meet you. I'm Leonard Smith," said the one with the wrist cuffs, his voice a mixture of Brooklyn and German.

She looked at him blankly.

After pausing for recognition, he added, "Still a no? … Fort Belvoir, remember?"

He was silent for a moment as it came back to her.

About a year earlier, Cindy uncovered a back door in the US Army's Fort Belvoir procurement operations center. Tracking the network traffic accessing and exiting the back door, she discovered a hacker was setting winning bids for DoD contracts by sabotaging competitive bids and fixing prices. Whoever it was, if he was working for just a 10 percent cut, had made himself more than $120 million during a period of two years before they caught up to him.

"The procurement hacker? That was you?" she asked, surprised.

"Well, I cannot confirm those claims, obviously," he answered, looking at the brass on either side of him. "I can say that everyone knows hacking into the DoD is trivial. But I'm glad to actually meet you. You have skills. By the way, how did you detect this so-called procurement hacker I'm accused of being?"

Confused, she turned back to her supervisor.

"Go ahead and answer. You have my permission to share your techniques related to this case," the colonel offered.

"Well, I noticed the traffic to your command-and-control server even though you tried to mask it. Then I started following it," Cindy explained cautiously so as not to give her techniques away. "While your crypto was hard to crack, we did finally get to see what you were doing."

"And that's one of the things we love about working with you, Cindy. You catch malicious patterns that our security intelligence and analytics tools can't detect," said Colonel James in his mentoring tone.

"Thank you, sir. But, sir, this is highly unusual for me to meet a suspect," she said. "Protocol dictates that I turn in my reports and deposit all evidence and forensics duplicates to the locker and then move on. So, I'm wondering what I'm doing here, sir."

"We'll get to that in a minute. First, here's a quick briefing on Leonard Smith," Colonel James said, handing her his iPad.

Cindy scanned the contents of the folders: child welfare documents showing that young Leonard was adopted by a well-to-do family, school and juvenile records showing he became a world-renowned hacker with the handle of StnKy (for stinky) by the age of thirteen, and warrants for arrest in his youth mostly for prank hacks, like screwing with the FBI.

"If you're at the part about the FBI," Leonard interjected, "those guys take themselves *far too seriously.*"

Cindy didn't disagree. But instead of commenting, she continued reading.

After turning nineteen and before being arrested again as an adult, Smith moved to Germany where there were no charges against him and started his own business, a managed security services company named Telecom Security Systems (TSS). TSS grew quickly and became the managed IT security provider to China Telecom with the motto Connecting the World. (China Telecom also had a US headquarters in Herndon, Virginia.) TSS also serviced Deutsch Telekom, among other large communications companies in Europe and Dubai. As such, Leonard ran a team of more than a thousand of the best cybersecurity and forensics experts in the world to monitor and protect his clients' networks.

After she finished reading the files, she looked up at her boss.

"I see he runs a legit business in addition to his illegal empire. What a surprise," she observed.

"Really? I was hoping you'd be impressed with my skills— you know, hacker to hacker," Leonard interjected.

Cindy tried to ignore him as she continued to press Colonel James. "But, sir, I'm still unclear what this has to do with me. And why wasn't his arrest ever in the news?" she inquired.

"We think Mr. Smith here could be of use to our department," he answered. "Given some of his TSS clients, Leonard here is an asset—"

"Are you saying you're trying to recruit *him?*" she interrupted, unbelieving. "From the background you just gave me, he's incorrigible. How can we even trust him not to continue hacking us?"

"Oh, so you *do* admire my skills," Leonard said, proudly. "But if it makes you feel any better, I'm not too happy about this 'deal' either. I'm only here because it lets me run TSS, and no employees lose their jobs. It also keeps me out of prison."

"So now you met me," she said and then stood to leave. "Sir, may I be excused?"

"Cindy, please take your seat again. We have business to discuss," Colonel James directed. He waited until she sat down again. "We need you to watch over his cyberactivities to make sure he's not selling us out or setting us up, that he's not counter spying. He will, of course, be chipped and monitored at all times."

"You want *me* to watch *him*?" she asked, incredulous. "I have so many better things to do than babysit a criminal—who should be serving twenty years for fraud by computer intrusion, by the way. Why not give the job to Max or Steve or any of the other excellent cybertalent we have?"

"This just got a whole lot more interesting," said Leonard, raising an eyebrow. "You've only got one life. Let your hair down, girl—literally. Live a little."

She resisted the urge to reach for her hair, which was pulled up in a tight bun.

"Sir, I cannot stress enough how exceedingly stealth this guy is. Watching over him will be a full-time job that will take an additional team and resources to analyze his claims and the data he'd be sending us. And it'd pull me off other important investigations," she argued.

"This is happening, Cindy," said Colonel James sternly. "For your cover, we'll be reassigning you to the NSA Signals Intelligence Division at Fort Meade. We have resources, staff, and technology already assigned to you."

"But, sir, I'm still working on the intrusion into the Air

Force Research Labs," she said. "I don't have time to reassign to SIGINT … I'm very close to discovering—"

"We've already reassigned that case," Colonel James interrupted. "Turn all your evidence into the locker and clean out your desk."

She paused a moment to think about her options. "Of course, I could refuse because I'm a contractor," she responded, a little too quietly.

"There *is* that option," James answered. "But consider that a nuclear option. Because if you don't accept the assignment, your contract with the DoD will be terminated."

An awkward moment passed as Leonard looked back and forth between them, wondering who would back down first.

"As you wish, sir," Cindy finally said. "And thank you for the assignment, Colonel. I won't let you down."

"I know you'll do a good job, Cindy," he replied, sounding fatherly again.

Then turning to the large man on his right, he added, "In fact, meet your new director from Fort Meade, General Greene."

She turned to the tall and dignified black man with a chest full of ranks and medals who'd been sitting expressionless throughout the conversation.

"Welcome to Fort Meade," said the general with a deep voice that bore a faint Texas accent.

Sliding a folder to her, he added, "Here are your assignment details and your upgraded security credentials. Please contact my office to go over your housing and other logistics."

CHAPTER 3.

BROKEN AND BLEEDING

PRESENT DAY

From her darkness, Cy hears Allure shouting and smells the meaty scent of blood. Des, barely conscious, lies on a transport gurney next to her, holding her hand. Someone's shouting at Med!c (for medic) to stop the bleeding—something about the aortic artery. Then, Cy fades out again.

They're in a makeshift operating room set up in an abandoned underground parking lot in Old Knoxville. It is humid and stuffy, and Allure, who's assisting Med!c, feels faint and sick to her stomach.

"The bullet went through his neck then it hit Cy in the back," Allure says emotionally. "I couldn't stop the blood."

Med!c, forty, is doctor to many of the hacker clans around the region, including Cy's clan. Born into a high-performing Asian family, he graduated early and accepted his residency at Stanford Hospital at age twenty-four where he, being an adrenalin junkie, spent most of his time between emergency, the ICU, and the brain trauma units. Then, for reasons only he knows, he removed his UI and walked away from a life of privilege, leaving behind very confused parents and a broken-hearted boyfriend.

Now, he's in this filthy fake operating room, flustered and sweating, with two of his best friends dying on either side of him. He's searching through a cache of small, embeddable chips that are wrapped in sterile packaging.

"Where the hell is Cy's UI?" he asks as he searches impatiently before finding Cy's chip beneath Allure's chip. "Ah, here it is. As close to a perfect match as we have."

The chips have all types of medical histories on them: type 1 and type 2 diabetes, a plethora of heart conditions, blood types, cancers, and other chronic conditions that they lifted from other peoples' UIs. This data is sorted and translated into chips that match the recipients' medical history so they can get the medicine and care they need.

"Are you saying we have to take them to the hospital?" Allure asks worriedly. "Won't they be *looking* for gunshot injuries?"

"It's the only choice we have if we want her to survive, let alone walk again," replies Med!c, pausing to think a moment. "I'm guessing Operation Backbone caused enough chaos to sneak in a gunshot wound under the radar."

"Latest report is that most auxiliary systems, including hospitals, cannot access the databases they need for positive verification," she answers. "And as you saw when you pulled in here, the roads are pretty shitty too ..."

"So the staff would have a hard time identifying and reporting new patients—even with a bullet wound," Med!c argues. "Remember, we planned for this ..."

Before Med!c finishes his sentence, Des gurgles alarmingly.

His chest rattles ominously. Then his grip on Cy's hand loosens, and her hand slips away.

For a moment, Allure and Med!c are silent, feeling the spirit of their beloved soldier linger and then leave the room. Allure breaks down first, blubbering like she'd never stop. Med!c, usually flippant and sacrilegious, places Des's dangling arm respectfully across his chest. Then he turns his attention back to Cy.

"What the *hell*? Cy? Cy?" he says.

"What now?" Allure asks, sniffling.

Cy, still unconscious, is silently weeping with tears pouring down her cheeks.

"Cy are you with us?" he asks.

Cy does not respond.

"Weird," he adds.

Taking in a deep breath, Med!c steels himself and continues with his plan. "We should slip her into the ER under the chaos," he says, a little teary-eyed. "We have the ambulance standing by, and we show up with forged papers, which will be impossible to verify since GlobeCom is down."

"OK, so what do you need me to do?" Allure asks.

"Go get Mane to prep the Humvee. I think he should bring Des back home, while you and I take Cy to St. Mary's Medical Center in La Follette. It's a Catholic hospital not affiliated with any of the military bases that may have old records with Cy's DNA ..."

Allure, eager to get out of the nauseating space, hurries off through their makeshift plastic barrier. She finds Mane in the back seat of the Humvee using his controller to update the vehicle's exterior camouflage. He takes one look at her face, sets down his controller, and opens his arms to her. She settles on the floor in between his legs as he embraces her. She buries her face on his barrel chest and lets the tears flow while he strokes her jet-black hair.

"Des is gone," she says with a great sob. "And, and ... We

don't know if Cy will make it, and if she does, will she ever walk again?"

Mane pulls her chin upward and looks in the large black pools of her eyes before kissing her lightly on the lips. Then he looks back into her eyes determinedly.

"Cy's strong. If anyone can get through this, she can," he says. "But ... I find it so ironic—"

"Don't even *say* it," Allure commands, trying to cut him off.

"It's just so damn ironic that she got shot in the back during an operation called Backbone," he observes.

"Jesus, why do you always have to *go* there?" she fires back.

Mane nuzzles her and rubs her shoulders. "You usually love how I state the obvious and the ironic," he responds.

"Well, this time I need to trust that you'll respectfully bring Des's body back home for a proper burial. Med!c and I need to get Cy to St. Mary's."

"You know I'll do that," he says, sounding a little offended. "I have nothing but respect for our fearless protector. I mean, this is *Des* we're talking about. He's legend. Sure, I was a pain in his ass, but I'm a royal pain in everyone's asses."

Allure reluctantly leaves Mane's embrace and grabs her things for the journey with Cy. She passes Skew and Elven as they work to change the labeling on Med!c's ambulance and stops to update them.

"Are they ... Are they OK?" asks a worried Elven, his voice both husky and slightly effeminate.

"We think we can save Cy. But"—she pauses, choking up before she collects herself—"I'm afraid we've lost Des ... We just couldn't stop the bleeding."

"No! Not Uncle Des!" Elven pleads before falling into his father's waiting arms. Skew, who is also teary-eyed, pats Elven's back, trying to comfort himself as much as his son.

"I'm sorry, my lad. Such a loss, such a good man," Skew says roughly. "He will be missed ... by all of us."

Allure is momentarily touched by the two men embracing—straight father and gay, mixed-race son who don't look in any way related.

"We need you to escort his body back to the ridge," Allure tells them. "Mane is driving, so you two control the scout drones. And he'd need your muscle for backup if he runs into problems."

"Yes, Mistress Allure," says Skew respectfully.

"Thank you ... both of you," she adds. "Now, I've got to get back to Cy. When you're done here, please finish our cleanup. Everything must be packed out of here and the whole area needs to look undisturbed."

Back inside the makeshift med room, Med!c has cleaned up and stuffed the bloody pads and sheets into plastic bags. He is mostly ready to go when Allure returns.

"Skew and team will clean the floors and then make them look dirty again after they get Des and his gurney in the Humvee," she says to Med!c as he wraps up.

"As they say, leave no trace," he replies. "We can't sterilize this place, but we can make it look like no one was ever here so as not to raise suspicion."

"Travel to St. Mary's will be a nightmare. We should take the back roads for as long as we can and avoid busy intersections and other places where dead smart vehicles are piled up," Allure advises.

"OK, I got that," replies Med!c. "And by the way, what about Cy's boys? Has anyone contacted them?"

Allure looks a little guilty.

"Um. The concern is that they'll do something stupid like try to visit their mom at the hospital, which we can't have ..." Allure hedges. "I mean, I feel bad, but before we embarked on the op, Cy made me promise to protect them if anything happened to her or Des ..."

"That's bad," Med!c shoots back. "At the very least, we need to send a message to Wizard. He'll know what to say to them and how."

SEVENTEEN YEARS EARLIER

Cindy got used to her new assignment at SIGNET, even grew to like it there. She soaked up information and learned world affairs while following the emerging powers of GlobeCom. Leonard Smith was stationed at China Telecom, which would soon become the China hub of GlobeCom as part of an international merger.

From Beijing, Leonard had been feeding her troubling news about the emergence of super networks connecting the global infrastructure in multicountry pacts and merging with GlobeCom. This was concerning because GlobeCom already owned the unique identifiers (UIs, which emerged out of the World Economic Forum in Davos). The UI chips, just a bit larger than a cooked grain of rice, were being inserted under the skin in people's left forearms to use in a variety of new applications from accessing medical services to buying dinner out and starting the car. Meanwhile, GlobeCom was also acquiring the largest social media platforms in the world.

Cy switched to a screen showing China Telecom was also planning a merger with Russian owned MTS (Mobile Telesystems), which had already merged with Deutsch Telekom to serve all of the EU and most of India. She had a sick feeling as she realized how thoroughly GlobeCom was dissolving the boundaries between public and private sectors and centralizing power through acquisition.

"So GlobeCom owns the network. And the data. And the unique identifiers implanted in all its human subjects," Cy said to herself as she read the news on her screens. "Can't anybody see what's going on here?"

She switched to her news feed and watched a clip about a fiery car crash in the French countryside.

"Investigators have determined that the car crash that took the life of Gabriel Dupres was caused by computer tampering. Someone remotely turned off steering to his smart car just as the car started into a sharp turn near his home in Bruyères-le-Châtel, France," said a female news anchor with a rich French accent.

"Dupres worked as chief investigator for Cyber Intelligence Gathering at the Centre de Calcul Recherche et Technologie, known as CCRT. He was on loan from the French Air Force, where he'd had a long and distinguished career in cybersecurity and red team hacking to find weaknesses in the French Air Force systems," the news anchor continued.

A still image showed Gabriel Dupres, a handsome mix of French and Persian, aged forty, dressed in a tuxedo and smiling next to his striking and sophisticated French Polynesian wife, Adrianna, thirty-eight. Adrianna, with light coffee-colored skin, was perfectly coifed in a sparkling gown with yellow and white diamonds on her ears and wrist. They held a beautiful, dark-skinned, mix-race toddler between them.

"Dupres is survived by his wife, a well-known philanthropist who is a member of the GlobeCom board of directors. He is also survived by their two-year-old son," the anchor concluded.

After viewing the newscast, Cindy called her lead intelligence officer into her office. "That case we assisted the French Air Force with just broke in the news. Can you come in for a quick debriefing?" she asked over the internal commline.

Her lead intelligence expert, a tall and gangly, black-skinned lieutenant with short-cropped hair, showed up a minute later viewing his iPad that was replaying the same news clip Cindy just watched.

"So, have you figured out why the attackers would leave traces of their malware behind but otherwise are completely invisible and impossible to track?" she asked.

"Well, we know that they got the malware into the auto maker's update systems, which then loaded into the car during a firmware update," he answered. "We know that only Mr. Dupres's car was altered even though the hack could have been used to control every one of those specific auto makes on the road. What we still don't know is who the perps were or where they came from."

Cindy nodded and then paused to think. "Well, the French Air Force won't give us any more access to their case file. They're pretty much done with us after we shared with them the manufacturer-to-vehicle connection," she said. "But I know there's more to this story ... Please continue searching our evidence anyway."

"Yes, ma'am," he said, making a note on his iPad.

"Also, I need an updated map on all the network hops that you tracked back from the auto manufacturer," she added.

After he left, Cindy returned to another of her computer screens and checked out an annual hacker conference happening in August in Las Vegas called bSides. One of the conference sessions caught her attention. It was titled, "Hacking Unique Identifiers for Fun and Profit."

She clicked the link to the session, and up popped a video of a hacker wearing a cow skull.

"Remember when GlobeCom announced to the world that their UIs were safe? That they were unhackable? That even the world's fastest multiprocessors couldn't crack their crypto?" he said, "Well, they were ..."

The words *WRONG, WRONG, WRONG* flashed across the screen in bold colors. Then the hacker in the cow skull continued talking.

"Come to the annual bSides conference in Vegas, where the

Cult of the Dead Cow will show you how to use someone else's so-called unique identifier to become them. Just think. Maybe you can become someone rich …"

Cindy was suddenly startled from her reading by General Greene, who was standing in her doorway.

"Good morning, Cindy," he said in his deep, commanding voice.

"Sir! I didn't hear you," she responded, turning to address him. "How long have you been there?"

"Long enough to see you still haven't updated your access credentials," he observed.

She subconsciously rubbed her left forearm where her UI would be implanted, saying, "Sir, this UI constitutes an invasion of my privacy. GlobeCom would be able to track everything I do."

"We've been through all this, Cindy," he answered, a little frustrated. "Researchers and policy experts at Davos spent years working on a secure unique identifier to give everyone unfettered and secure access to digital records. The chips are unhackable."

"Unhackable. I've heard that before—pretty much every time we adopt a shiny new tech. And always, it gets hacked," she argued. "In fact, I'm reading about a session at bSides where—"

"Decision's final," he said, shutting her down. "One month from today, you'll need to have your UI to get into the building, the same as every other person working here."

Cindy held back a growing urge to hurl. She sighed and then answered grudgingly, "Yes, sir. I'll go to the registrar next week."

"Good. I knew you'd see reason," he said.

As soon as he left her office, Cindy pulled her waste bin between her knees and promptly threw up. She emptied it into the toilet in the bathroom across from her office and washed up. Then she looked at herself carefully in the mirror, pulling her white blouse tight over her belly to reveal a small but growing baby bump. Now in her second trimester, it would be harder to hide her condition.

"Don't worry, little baby," she said to her belly. "Nobody knows about you, and I won't let them put a chip implant in you without your knowledge or permission."

A week later, Cindy's coworkers crowded in her office, mugs of morning coffee in their hands. The military clock above her desk read 07:15, and Cindy was nowhere to be found.

"She's never late, so I had to check," said one coworker, a male in his thirties. "Unfortunately, I don't think we'll ever see her again."

They were all looking at her screensavers, which played the opening scene from *The Hitchhiker's Guide to the Galaxy* where the dolphins left the planet by floating up to the sky. Over the floating dolphins, she had superimposed this message: *"SO LONG, AND THANKS FOR ALL THE PHISH."*

CHAPTER 4.

ORDER TO CHAOS

PRESENT DAY

Dead smart cars are piled up like trash along the roadsides as Allure steers the ambulance down an abandoned side road toward St. Mary's Hospital in Lafayette. Med!c tends the still unconscious Cy on the gurney in the back.

Allure slows to navigate a four-way intersection for her right turn onto Long Hollow Road. Vehicles of all types are abandoned on the curbs and side streets with comatose traffic lights hanging uselessly overhead.

"It's kind of a shit show out here," she says, projecting her voice so Med!c can hear from behind. "But looks like most vehicles failed safely. Even the pileups in the intersection don't look exceptionally deadly ..."

"So, not *too bad?*" Med!c asks, a hint of sarcasm in his voice.

"Yeah. Uh, I mean no. I mean, it shouldn't have been this bad," she responds.

At that moment, the CB radio in her pocket crackles, and a female voice signs on. "Ninety percent effective. Repeat, 90 percent," the voice says. "Look to the sky for the other 10 percent."

"Shit!" Allure exclaims. "Will those things start falling from the sky?"

"Um, I don't think so," says Med!c, as he moves to the back window and looks up just in time to see a quick yellow-orange flash in the deep blue afternoon sky. "Of course, I could be wrong."

"What'd you see?" she asks.

"I discerned what looked like a tiny yellow spark," he answers, still looking up. "Based on the color, it was probably a low-orbit observation satellite hit by a ground laser."

"Well it couldn't have been a plane," Allure responds, hoping she's right. "As long as the pilots have been trained properly, they should be able to land with line of sight, radios, and manual controls."

Looking out the window at the mess on the roadway behind him, Med!c doubts that anything landed, stopped, or ended safely.

Allure, uncomfortable with his silence, continues. "Everything should soon switch to local systems," she adds. "The road and vehicle sensors will hand off directly to each other without the need to go through GlobeCom central data hubs. The only problem is the mapping."

"Well, the most recent geolocation data is stored in the municipal systems and the vehicles themselves," he acknowledges. "But do you-all think that these municipalities are going to make the transition to local systems and supply chains?"

"Well, they'd need to resurrect their old cell towers, which we've already been using for clan messaging, so they are all operational," she explains. "It should take about a week to transition to local data, transport, and sensory systems, I would think."

"So, not centralized but localized," he surmises.

"Yes," she affirms. "They used to do networking this way until about fifteen years ago with pretty good success."

Allure abruptly stops talking as she pulls into St. Mary's emergency vehicle waiting area.

The scene is chaos. Vehicles are lined up three wide and four deep with nurses admitting and triaging new patients out on the sidewalk.

"What happened to do no harm?" asks Med!c, who's looking over Allure's shoulder at the mayhem.

"Um, out of chaos will come order?" Allure answers, a little unsure. "Eventually?"

"Don't worry. I've got this," he says as he grabs some printed papers and steps into the fray.

Outside the van, he raises the papers over his head, shouting over the din.

"Gunshot victim, forty-six-year-old female, blood loss but stabilized; bullet lodged in lower thoracic spine … *We have insurance papers!*" he announces.

Nearly twenty hours later, Cy wakes without stirring in a recovery room at St. Mary's surgical department. Remaining still and from behind her closed eyes, she observes that she is in a real hospital, hooked to IVs. She sees she is also being transfused! For a moment, she feels panic start to undo her. What if they gave her the wrong blood type? Of course, she'd already be dead by now if that were the case. The realization calms her, and she continues to fake sleep as she evaluates her surroundings.

They must have matched her information and blood type to someone else's UI, which means she'd have an embedded chip in her arm with medical information matching hers. Concentrating, she could feel it there, a newly inserted UI just beneath her skin and above the wrist of her left forearm, burning a little.

Over the soft beeping and chiming from her monitors, she hears Med!c talking to a doctor about a patient named Martha and her release from recovery to the spinal unit at another hospital in Knoxville. The tending surgeon is referring to Med!c as Dr. Yee.

"We know it's early, but we'll have to release her tomorrow," says the tending surgeon in a deep male southern voice. "We, unfortunately, need the bed."

"I can see you do. It's been crazy around here since GlobeCom crashed," says Med!c empathetically, acting as Dr. Yee. "Any idea when you'll have at least the local systems back online?"

"I don't know. I'm not in that department. But it's been hell, that's for sure," the surgeon answers.

"Oh, that reminds me. Any status on the police report?" Med!c asks.

"We wrote the report and collected the evidence, but there's no way to get it to the police station right now with the comms down. All we can do is put police-related information on a bulletin board for when they stop by."

"So old-school! Creative, though," says Med!c as Dr. Yee.

"Thanks, Doctor, for your help with the overflow patients during this past twenty-four hours," says the surgeon, who's truly appreciative. "Not all MDs would leave their own practice to step in during emergencies like this."

"The least I could do. Besides, I was stuck here once I came in to check on Martha," Med!c answers. "I didn't really want to face that chaos on the road, but now the roads seem to be opening up a bit."

Once the room finally clears of doctors and nurses and their sounds fade away down the hallway, Cy whispers to Med!c. "Where are we?" she asks hoarsely. "And why ... Why can't I feel my legs?"

Feeling a bit guilty, he covertly injects more sedative in her drip line, keeping his actions out of view of the cameras. He then strokes her graying hair as she drifts off again.

"Sleep, dear lady," he says quietly. "We will answer your questions soon, but we can't have you getting all hysterical before we bust you out of here."

SEVENTEEN YEARS EARLIER

Leonard anxiously paced his penthouse suite at the Watergate Hotel, pausing intermittently to look out the picture window at a wide view of the Potomac River before resuming his pacing again. Absently, he scratched his left forearm above his wrist where his implant itched.

When he heard the expected knock at his door, he shut a silver-colored clamshell carry case on the coffee table and then excitedly hurried to the door.

Cindy was in his arms before it closed behind them.

"It's been too long, too long. I've missed you," he said, kissing her face, her mouth, hungrily.

"I've missed you too, my love, my darling," Cindy responded, holding him tight against her heart and kissing him back just as ardently.

As they embraced, his hand instinctively slipped down to her stomach.

"How's my DNA? Is he kicking yet?" he asked.

"It's my DNA also, don't forget," she answered breathily. "But no kicking yet. It's still early. And we have no idea if it's a *he* yet, either."

All the time Leonard was acquiring land trusts and shell companies to hide his ill-gotten fortune, he hadn't realized, until now, that he'd been doing all of this to help her and this child of theirs to start a new life off the grid. The things that could go wrong made him shudder. He hoped he'd thought of everything they would need to thrive.

Leonard kissed Cindy again with growing urgency before steering her gently to the bed, slowly peeling off her clothing and kissing each part of her skin that he exposed.

"You've gotten softer—and fuller—here and here," he said, nuzzling her breast and caressing her hip. "I like it."

Their lovemaking was heartfelt, lustful, and precious as it always was—even more intense for Cindy with her hormones raging. They dined off one another in their big bed. They made love in the shower, on the bed, on the loveseat. He made her swoon, and she made him breathless, and they knew it would always be this way on the rare occasions when they could be together.

When they were finally sated, Cindy and Leonard cuddled on the loveseat in their hotel robes, empty food plates on the table. It was near dawn, and they took this time to talk shop.

"Well, the news is out: Gabriel Dupres's accident was no accident," she started. "Authorities are saying freedom-fighting hackers are the ones who rigged his car, but we can't tell who did it or where they came from."

"I've got some troubling news for you too, and it may be related to your case," Leonard responded. "I'm being watched very closely by one of the GlobeCom twenty-four. And I'm pretty sure it's Strand."

"You mean, Damian Strand, head of the board of directors? Head of the twenty-four?" she asked, unpinning her arm from under his neck and turning toward him to look him in the eyes.

"That's the one," he said, adjusting himself to face her.

"How the hell did you catch *his* attention?" she asked worriedly.

"I'm not sure," Leonard answered. "I'm meticulous, as you

know, and there are no indicators he's onto my more, *ahem*, clandestine activities."

"You're not *that* meticulous," she challenged. "I caught you in DoD systems, as you recall. Maybe he's onto you and looking to see how he can profit from your nefarious activities!"

"Yeah, well that was then, and this is now," Leonard responded, smiling at the memory of meeting her. "As Leonard Smith, I've evolved to live my online life in the open, fitting into the algorithms of GlobeCom uniformity. Finding my other activities under my d_ArkAngl persona would be like searching for ghosts that don't exist."

"So then, why is Strand so interested in you?" she asked again.

"It may be because Strand doesn't trust someone with US citizenship managing security for China's largest networking company. Or it could be what I found in my daily log dump from the French CCRT."

"What about the log dumps?" she asked. "Maybe you should have *led* with that."

"I saw that someone using Gabriel Dupres's unique identifier had downloaded an encrypted file off of one of Strand's systems not more than twenty-four hours before Dupres was killed in that staged car accident," he explained. "It was a very large file—in the petabytes."

"What? Why would you be collecting the logs from CCRT traffic when it's not in the eastern territory covered by your hub in Beijing?" she asked.

"Good question. I was involved because I'm supervising the technical due diligence for the merger between GlobeCom and the CCRT," he explained. "Dupres was working for me. I asked him to start by validating the security controls of the CCRT."

"Ooooooh shit. That's not good," Cindy said, shaking her head, realization dawning.

"But it gets deeper," he continued. "Dupres's wife, Adrianna, was instrumental in convincing the CCRT to merge with GlobeCom in the first place, essentially handing GlobeCom the keys to the all the observation powers and tools owned by the CCRT."

"I saw that on my feed," Cindy noted. "Adrianna's grieving and pissed, so she's pushing for stiff sentences, even the death penalty, for hacking into GlobeCom systems. It looks like the headline here is, 'Strand manipulates a wounded widow to do his bidding.'"

"Something like that," Leonard agreed. "And I'm guessing it's a win in Strand's larger game to control everything."

"So, what about your safety? What did you do with the log dump?" she asked, suddenly worried again.

"The logs don't have any evidence of *what* was in the file that Dupres transferred, just that something big *was* transferred," Leonard answered. "Not enough to risk my life over, so I erased all traces. If Strand finds anything, he would think I was covering his back, and that could make him finally trust me."

"Good!" she said, pulling him close and laying her head in the crook of his neck.

"Come with me—with us?" she asked. "It would be better than staying behind in a hostile world with GlobeCom always watching and pulling your strings."

"I let GlobeCom see what I want them to see and no more," d_ArkAngl replied. "I wish I could go with you, but I must stay where I'm at. I'm more effective as a privileged GlobeCom insider than a thousand hackers are on the outside."

She was quiet a moment, her brow creasing like it did when she tried to solve hard problems.

"I have a present for you. A little something to help keep you safe," Leonard offered, hoping to cheer her up.

He pulled the clamshell case closer to them on the coffee table and opened it to reveal a realistic-looking white Scottish Terrier.

"Oh, a little robot dog!" she exclaimed. "What's its name?"

"His name is R3x. That's *R*, the number three, *X*," he said. "All he can do is authenticate people coming on your property for now. But he's programmable, and I'm guessing over time you'll find other uses for him."

She switched on R3x's power button behind his head, and R3x let out a sharp little bark.

"When it barks, you authenticate by creating your own pass-code with your voice. Then you need to repeat that same passcode each time you reauthenticate," Leonard explained.

"Red Rover, red Rover, red Rover all over," she recited to R3x, who wagged his tail, seeming pleased.

"No, no, that won't work. He will need different words, sounds, and tones so he can get a good read on your voice. Try another passphrase," Leonard instructed.

"What would happen if a person failed authentication with R3x, and I'm not there to verify them?" she asked.

"That's when he'd send live feed video to you … and to your security detail," he explained.

"Cool. Um, wait," she said. "I have a security detail?"

"I'm working on that," he answered.

CHAPTER 5.

HIDING IN CHAOS

PRESENT DAY

Allure is waiting behind the wheel in a white emergency transport van with a green logo that reads: "Tennessee Brain and Spinal Injury Rehabilitation Center." She's tapping her long fingers to the historic Beatles song, "Revolution," a special selection from her stored music groupings.

There's no doubt that the local police will catch up with Cy, the gunshot victim at the spinal facility, even with GlobeCom down. So, they decided to act during Cy's transfer and instead bring her home for rehab.

Allure looks up from her steering wheel and sees a plump, redheaded nurse pushing Cy in a compact transport gurney toward her van. The nurse's pink skin glistens with sweat, and she looks exhausted.

Allure jumps out to lend a hand, looking the part of a tall, thin orderly in khakis with her company logo on the sleeve of her polo-style shirt. Allure's name badge with the same logo reads: "Sandra Smith, EMT and Orderly."

"Let me get that for you," Allure offers, taking the gurney from the nurse and steering it around to the back of the van where she opens the doors and lowers the ramp.

"Thank—thank you," says the nurse who's more than happy to hand the burden over.

"Long day?" asks Allure, playing the part of sympathetic peer.

"Y'all have no idea. Or maybe you do," says the nurse in a rich Georgian accent. "Everything's been crazy since GlobeCom went down. All our beds are filled with accident victims because, apparently, folks can't drive around here in a manual car anymore. But I see y'all can."

"Can what?" Allure asks absently as she locks Cy's gurney into the back of the van.

"Drive," the nurse repeats.

"Oh, yes. Dad taught me to drive when I was fifteen," responds Allure, who finds it easier to make up stories on the fly by sticking close to the truth. "It was a stick shift, otherwise known as a manual drive."

"I've heard some of them manual vehicles are still on the road today," the nurse replies.

"Guilty!" Allure says, pointing to herself. "I have an old Ford pickup at home that I race around our farm just for the hell of it sometimes."

The nurse smiles at the thought, a diversion from her current crazy workload. Allure changes the subject back to the patient.

"We usually take them once they're sitting up and awake," Allure says, still acting as the orderly.

"Right. She should even be in PT by now, but she's been

sleeping this whole time," the nurse answers. "We think she was oversedated, or else she just heals by sleeping a lot."

"OK, so that's why she's still on the IV?" asks Allure.

The nurse nods affirmatively, adding, "Hydration and electrolytes. She needs to eat soon ... Here's her paperwork and her things."

"Papers?" Allure asks, feigning surprise. "We're back in the dark ages!"

Allure quickly looks over the medical summary in the file: The bullet shattered Cy's T-7. The surgeons implanted a new disk and reestablished many of the nerve pathways, but the damage was extensive. The neurostimulator will connect the broken nerves, and she will need rigorous therapy.

"The cooler contains the evidence, so keep it on ice until the police catch up with this case please," the nurse adds.

"Hopefully, things will get easier for you," Allure offers as she climbs back into the driver's seat.

The nurse waves goodbye as Allure slowly drives away.

Two hours later, Cy's eyes flutter open to see Allure's worried face frowning down on her.

"Thank *God* you're finally awake! I was so worried!" exclaims Allure.

"Welcome back, sleepyhead," Mane says from the driver's seat of the van as he slowly weaves the vehicle through the forested path toward their home base.

Cy recognizes that they are already on the eastern edge of their property, so they will be home within the hour. She tries to speak, but her mouth is too dry. Allure puts a straw to her lips. Cy drinks heavily, and Allure slows her down so she won't get sick.

"How … How long have I been out?" Cy croaks hoarsely. "And why am I strapped down?"

"Well, it's a totally crazy story," says Mane excitedly. "I mean, you can't make this shit up."

"Mane, darling, remember you were going to let me tell Cy what happened, like we rehearsed," Allure reminds him.

"Oh. Yeah, OK. Sorry. It's just so fucking unreal," he says. "Go on, go on. I'll shut up."

"First, we need you to sit up. So now that you're awake, I'm going to adjust your gurney position," Allure starts.

She slowly raises the back of the gurney until Cy is sitting up.

"So, you've been out for two and a half days. You were treated at St. Mary's Hospital under an assumed identity."

"It must have been bad if I'm still in a gurney," Cy observes. "What happened to me?"

"We thought we were in the clear, but you got shot in the back," Allure answers. "As you climbed into the Humvee, your flak vest hiked up enough to expose your T-7, which was shattered by a bullet from a rogue drone."

"So that's why I woke up in a hospital," Cy says, feeling less confused.

"Oh? You woke up?" Allure asks.

"Yes, when Med!c was there," Cy answers.

Allure recalls the nurse telling her Cy had possibly been asleep the whole time and overmedicated but doesn't say anything. She makes a note to ask Med!c about this the next time she sees him.

"Unfortunately, you're paralyzed from the waist down—but we don't think that will be forever," Allure continues. "That's why we took you to the hospital—for their state-of-the-art nanotech that we simply don't have."

"OK. I suspected something like that, given I can't feel my legs but everything above the waist hurts like hell," Cy answers soberly.

"We expect the neuro implants to re-create your nerve pathways. You should walk again," Allure offers.

Mane, who's driving, can't contain himself any longer. "It's lost on nobody that you were shot in the back during Operation Backbone. It's just so damn ironic," he says.

Cy ignores him as she looks out the window at the dappled afternoon light blinking past them.

"And where … Where is Des?" she asks, suddenly worried. "Did he get out safe? Is he with the boys?"

"The boys are at home. They have everything all ready for you," Allure says, choking up a little. "They are amazing. You know, they are actually building you some leg supports on the 3D …"

For a second, Cy's heart warms at the image of her sons taking such initiative … and then it chills to ice because they still haven't answered her question about Des.

"And Des?" Cy demands. "Where is he? *Where the hell is Des?*"

Allure takes Cy's hands in hers and looks her straight in the eyes, tears welling. "I'm so sorry. We tried to save him …"

Cy starts crying and yelling hysterically. "No, no, no, *nooo.*"

Allure and Mane remain quiet as she unleashes her anguish and finally cries herself out. Cy, drained, is calmer but still crying a little when Mane decides enough time has passed for him to tell his version of the story.

"What's really twisted is that you were both hit by the *same bullet.* It passed through his neck, severing an artery, and then out the other side before lodging into your spine. Damndest thing."

Cy withdraws her hand from Allure's. She feels small and broken without Des.

"Now hang in there, girl. Remember, you're a badass mother fucker … You just survived a bullet in your back," Mane offers, sensing her weakness.

"I don't feel like a badass. I feel like I'm in some alternate universe that changed overnight—a universe that I've got no control over," Cy says helplessly.

"The whole world changed for everybody the moment we broke GlobeCom," Allure agrees. "Nobody has control right now."

After another pause, Mane clears his throat to update Cy on Des.

"We had to bury Des while you were in hospital—for practical reasons. Sorry," he says.

"He's in his favorite place. We're hoping for a service at the gravesite as soon as you are able, if that's OK with you," adds Allure helpfully. "Pri3st would like to preside. They're thinking sunset ..."

Cy closes her eyes and opens them again to look out the window at the vivid fall colors blurring past. "He always loved this time of year on the ridge," she says, her voice far away.

"And he would want you to keep on living and keep on fighting," Allure challenges. "He wouldn't want you wallowing in grief and giving up the fight because of him."

Cy pushes a slight smile through her tears and recites their go-to pep phrase. "Never give up. Never give in," she says, her voice still small and quiet.

"Never give up. Never give in," repeat Allure and Mane with much more conviction in their voices.

SEVENTEEN YEARS EARLIER

After leaving d_ArkAngl behind at the Watergate, Cindy officially became CyAnthia, Cy for short. This was her given hacker handle, and from that moment forward, Cindy Frank no longer existed.

Soon, Cy was winding her way up the Allegheny Mountains in a refurbished 2005 Jeep Cherokee. She chose the vehicle because it was low-tech (and thus untrackable) and because it was an indestructible workhorse built for the type of terrain where she would be living.

She passed the Homestead Hot Springs Resort and continued for another fifteen miles on the 220. Then she turned onto Mountain Valley Road, drove two more miles, and started looking for the unmarked dirt road she was directed to. When she found it, she had to park the car and open three rusty locked gates about twenty feet apart from one another and separated by cattle guards. She walked gingerly over the cattle grates trying not to sprain an ankle and used the color-coded keys d_ArkAngl had given her to open the gates. Once she had the final gate locked behind her, she followed the small green triangles painted on the trees pointing the way.

There were no roads, no tire marks, and the triangles were undiscernible if you didn't know what you were looking for. The property had to appear unlived in, so as not to raise interest of outsiders. It also needed to be inhospitable to hunters, hence the no trespassing and no hunting signs (you are being watched), rusted gates, cattle grates, obviously placed observation cameras, and old barbwire fencing.

"Everything but a moat," Cy said to herself at one point in the journey.

That wasn't entirely true she found out, as she also ended up forging two creeks, one of which came almost up to her floorboard.

From the moment she went off-road, Wizard, fifty-three, watched her from remote cameras hidden in the trees. As he prepared to meet her, he turned around to check himself in the mirror and make sure he was presentable.

"I used to be quite the catch," he said aloud to himself in a strong British accent. "I'm not all that anymore ..."

His hair grayed early into a dirty-looking yellow that matched his unkempt yellowing fingernails, neither of which he seemed to notice. He kept his hair long, and with his lean, tall frame, he looked almost the classic image of the old wizard.

Thirty minutes later, Wizard was waiting for Cy as she pulled up to a sod-roof garage that was sprouting small trees up top. He was dressed casually in khaki hiking shorts and a white cotton shirt and muddy boots with his skinny legs bulging at the knees.

As she pulled in, Cy noticed that the back end of the double-deep garage was full of supplies—racks stacked with fuel barrels, cans of car oil and other fluids, tools (including a tractor and a jackhammer), fencing, a cement mixer, and building materials. It looked to Cy like d_ArkAngl and Wizard had thought of every building, transportation, and repair need they'd have for living in the mountains.

She climbed out of the car and Wizard happily greeted her.

"Hellooo, hellooo! Mistress CyAnthia. I hope you had safe travels," Wizard said in his scholarly sounding British voice.

"Hello, you must be Wizard," she said, shaking his hand. "Please just call me Cy."

"Yes, Mistress Cy."

"No. Just Cy, thank you. I am no den mom," she repeated.

"Not yet, you're not … But you and I will be vetting new recruits in a short time," he replied.

Cy, uncomfortable with the discussion, changed the subject. "Looks like you have quite the resources—enough to keep things together for the long haul."

"You might say that," Wizard answered. "This is but one of many survival locations we have around the world, you know, in case we need to move in a hurry."

Trying to help, he grabbed the first bag he reached, but its weight surprised him. "Wow, much heavier than it looks," he said, straining to pull it out without dropping it.

"Oh, that," she responded. "That contains my book of gold coins—the trade-in value of all my belongings and assets. Not much, sadly, but gold is heavy. d_ArkAngl said to bring them. We'll need them for trading."

"He left a lot more trading bling than what's in this bag for us, mistress," Wizard said. "Some at your place, some at mine, and some hidden in the caves between us."

"Good to know," she noted before looking down at his muddy boots.

"Oh. Sorry for the mess. Right before you pulled in, we had a microstorm that dumped two inches in ten minutes," he explained.

"Strange … It wasn't raining where I was driving."

"Like I said, microstorm," he repeated.

She took two more duffle bags and the case with R3x and then followed Wizard, careful to avoid puddles along the way. Once past the garage, the trees opened up into a small but sunny glen with a spring in the middle.

"Welcome to your new home," he said, gesturing around like a ringmaster.

"Home? Where? I don't see anything," she said, looking puzzled.

"Exactly the point, mistress," he answered, proud of himself. "I should have said, 'Welcome to your hideaway.'"

They passed the spring and continued toward the rocks.

"That's a cold spring and good drinking water. They mostly have hot springs around here—one of the reasons we chose this area," he explained as they continued across the soggy ground. "The hot springs really screw up heat seekers, not to mention they make good geothermal sources of power."

Just past the glen up against the rock outcropping was an old lean-to and an outdoor distillery half covered in vines that looked more than a hundred years old—and probably was.

"I'm sure I could put that still to good use," joked Cy.

"I was hoping you'd say that," Wizard said, winking.

When she looked closer at the lean-to, she realized some of the vines were artfully applied to camouflage a hidden front door. Wizard gave it a tug and let her in ahead of him.

"It's like the TARDIS in here!" she said, surprised at the room's size.

To that, Wizard stood a little straighter, even more pleased with himself.

"The illusion is created by the rock backdrop," he explained.

He escorted her through an empty ten-by-ten-foot space that butted up to a steep granite cliff face, much like a miner's entrance in front of a cave during the gold rush, minus the rail tracks.

"Although this room appears to be empty, we are actually being monitored and authenticated before we get through the next door," he added.

"Door?" she asked. "All I see is solid rock at the end of the lean-to."

Wizard pulled a lever, and some of the rock wall, which was fake and made of painted foam to match the granite around it, lifted upward, revealing a double-reinforced steel panic door.

"You can leave this up most of the time," he said of the faux rock wall. "Currently, authentication is all voice recognition because we keep no database of faces."

"OK. That's how R3x does it too," she replies.

"Rex?" Wizard asked, raising a hairy eyebrow.

"Tell you later," she said, patting her clamshell case.

"All the doors are designed to lock from the inside so that you cannot lock yourself in, but you can lock yourself out," Wizard continued. "To get in you will always need the command code. To get out, you can just push the button."

"OK, good to know," she noted.

"After I give you the tour, you can program your own pass-phrase in. Until then, we use mine," he continued.

Turning to the microphone, he spewed a burst of zeros and ones in seven-bit integers followed by the words to an old R.E.M. song.

"It's the end of the world as we know it, and I feel fine."

The thick metal door swung inward.

"Did you just speak in ASCII?" she asked, surprised. "That code's so old it started with the telegraph."

When the door opened, they entered a naturally formed ter-race surrounded with an ornate wrought iron railing to prevent people from falling off the edge. On their left was a spiral stair-case carved from the rock leading downward. Embedded LED lighting at the baseboards illuminated the stairs, resembling large, uncut diamonds. Next to the stairs was a dumbwaiter, able to lift up to a thousand pounds from the looks of it.

Wizard sat down on a bench by the door and removed his muddy boots, dropping them in a wooden crate sitting beside the bench. She sat next to him and quietly did the same.

"Babies can make us do extreme things, can't they, mistress?" he said gently. "But don't worry, you can't be in better company."

"Do you have any children?" she asked.

"Nay, that was not in my cards, although there could be a lad or two I don't know about," he answered wistfully. "I think of your d_ArkAngl as my son, you know. I suppose that makes you my daughter-in-law."

In a hurry to see the source of light beyond the railing, Cy set out too fast in her stocking feet and ended up sliding part of the way across the polished granite floor.

"We'll need some type of floor mat to keep people from flying over the rail," she said.

When she reached the rail, she looked straight down into a great room. The twenty-foot-high, jagged rock ceiling above a large round table was embedded with lights in a colored, swirling pattern reminiscent of Vincent van Gogh's *The Starry Night*.

"Wow, you've been busy with the place. It looks amazing. I *love* the lighting," she exclaimed.

"d_ArkAngl thought you'd like that and said he's one of your favorite artists. Adjustable lighting will be of utmost importance living underground," Wizard gushed. "Most of this place already existed as an old dwelling for some moonshiners. Geothermally powered. And your air filtration system is so good that you could survive a nuclear war down here."

"Let's hope it never comes to that," she said under her breath.

"We should start with the kitchen," he advised as he led her down the stairs. "We can get your things later. Just leave them here for now."

There was a full working kitchen directly in front of the round table and then a hallway and other rooms that branched off from there, each its own misshapen space that reminded Cy of a luxury version of the Flintstones dwellings.

When they got to the large bathroom, Cy was truly impressed.

"That tub looks almost like a heart, and the spigot like a waterfall. Is it funneling the hot spring water?" she asked.

"Hot, cold, and in between. A whole-house water filtration system takes out the microbes, and a cold-water mixer prevents tap temperature from scalding anyone," Wizard explained.

"And how did you get a skylight in here?" she asked.

"The skylight is really just a tunnel through the rocks with reflective coating and a plexiglass top to keep out the elements," he answered.

She paused to look into a supply room with enough rations, diapers, tech equipment, medical kits, linens, baby and work clothing, etc. to last several years.

"So, you two figured we'll be in this for the long haul, I see," she said. "And I'm guessing we're planning on sharing some of these supplies with others, as needed?"

"You figured correctly, mistress. But we also know that you like to garden and have skills in animal husbandry. We planned on that fresh food as well," he said. "I myself want to raise chickens on my property and am nearly finished with the coop."

Cy raised a brow, impressed. "So what about bears? Won't they be eating the chickens?"

"Bears sleep through the winter, and our bear-resistant fencing *should* do the job the rest of the year. But for good measure, I've got electric wire to shock the bears before they get close to the fencing," he said. "And motion-sensor lights have been scaring them off pretty good so far."

"We're gonna need more than that, I'm guessing," she replied.

"We have weapons for any kind of incursion, including unruly bears," he added. "Do you know how to use them? I ask because I don't."

"I know how to shoot a target or a downed animal like a horse with a broken leg," she said. "Never trained to shoot moving targets, though. I'd have to learn."

Next, he showed her the computer workroom.

Several curved display monitors were spread across a half dozen work desks lit by hanging overhead spotlights in the eighteen-by-twenty-foot space. Like the other rooms, the walls were uneven granite that was smooth in some places and jagged in others. In front of the back wall, floor-to-ceiling metal racks were stocked with electronic components. The smaller parts like cables, batteries, and chips were piled in empty milk crates. Soldering tools, wire clippers, screwdrivers, duct tape, and other tools of the trade were also organized on the shelves, along with server hardware and other componentry. On the floor, two wall-mount display monitors leaned against the work desks for support.

"Oh, the things I can do with this space to make it my perfect lair!" she said excitedly as she looked around. "I can see putting one of those monitors over the doorway here and facing the work-stations to look straight at it."

"We have an encrypted private network with low-signal tow-ers set up across the property," he added. "It's good enough to fully cover our ten thousand acres."

"Will we be able to update those tower signals to block drone visuals of our above-ground activities, like farming and moving around?" Cy asked. "Because I anticipate flyovers from GlobeCom's observation drones."

"Already working on that," Wizard answered. "Right now, we're not seeing any overhead surveillance, partly due to our prox-imity to the Homestead Hot Springs Resort, which is a designated no-fly zone. But that will change in the future as GlobeCom ex-pands its reach. By then, we will be ready with the right signal scramblers and fake image renditioning to make this property seem uninhabited to flyovers."

"So, they'll see what we want them to see—an empty and wild ridge instead of visual signs of our activities like gardens and chicken coops," she repeated to make sure she got it right. "And you can make these images change with the seasons?"

"That's right, mistress."

Off the hall, she also spotted two undefined empty spaces about eight feet long, ten feet tall, and six feet deep, like bed-sized cubbies in the wall.

"You could make mini bedrooms out of those spaces, just put in a cot behind a curtain," she said. "Or a set of twin bunks even."

"Hadn't thought of that, but it is a good use of those spaces— if you ever need the extra beds, that is," he said encouragingly. "I do know that a woman's touch will be nice around here."

"Are you kidding me? You've done fabulous so far," she said, meaning it. "It's like you both thought of everything. It hardly feels like we're underground."

"Making you and that babe as comfortable as possible here—d_ArkAngl was adamant about that," Wizard responded.

"And let me guess … That's the master bedroom," she said, poking her head into one of the bedrooms off the hall. "I love the woven willow baby bassinette by the bed. Was it made locally?"

"Yes, mistress. Less than twenty miles from here, actually, from a wood working studio near the homestead. Now, let me take you to the rear emergency exit."

The hallway ended with another panic door embedded into the rock. Wizard pushed a button at eye level. The door swung out to a large cavern, overhead lights automatically turning on. She stepped back, surprised. Dark, foamy water, like frothing chocolate milk, roared through the cavern below them.

"The fork to the right leads to my small and humble abode, about a quarter mile in a winding tunnel, mostly walkable. But in some places, you have to duck or do the mambo," he pointed out.

Looking at the water warily, Cy asked, "How would I even go through there without drowning? There's so much rushing water."

"You're right. You should never go in there when it looks like this. It could wash you to another state," he agreed. "Normally there's dry ground to walk on and no water running in here, but we just had this microstorm."

"That's why this door appears to be watertight?" she asked.

"It *is* watertight," he assured her. "And we put the controller up high at eye level so that no little kiddies could accidentally open it."

"Note to self: keep this door locked at all times," Cy said aloud.

Wizard laughed lightly and put his arm around her shoulder. "We are going to make great friends, you and I."

CHAPTER 6.

HOMECOMING

PRESENT DAY

Mane drives carefully past the garage and around the edge of the soggy glen. Then he rolls to a stop in front of a hastily built wheelchair ramp out front of the lean-to. Cy, now in a wheelchair and looking out her window, can see her sons waiting on the ramp as they approach. So strong. So brave. And so lost. Men, not boys.

At six foot one, Michael, sixteen, is two inches taller and more muscular than his older brother, Adam, seventeen. Michael stands straight and looks well put together, while Adam appears disheveled, as if he just woke up. Like his father, Des, Michael has hazel eyes, although his brown hair comes from Cy's side. Adam's steel-blue eyes and strawberry-blond hair take after his real father, d_ArkAngl.

Cy feels the familiar pang of guilt about not telling Adam that

49

d_ArkAngl is his genetic parent. She sighs worriedly, so Allure places a comforting hand on her shoulder.

"It'll be OK," Allure says, coaching her. "You have your hands, your brains. That doesn't change how you love them or how they love you. The rest will follow."

When the van stops, Adam and Michael bound down the ramp and greet their mother at the back doors of the van. Unable to wait, Adam climbs in and throws his arms around Cy while kneeling on the floorboard.

"Mom! We were so worried about you," he manages to choke out. "And ... Dad ..."

His words fail. Cy pats him gently, closes her eyes, breathes him in, and swallows her tears. She must be strong for her sons.

"I know, I know. I'm OK. I'll be OK. I was worried about you too," Cy responds, looking over Adam's shoulder at Michael, who's standing ready to assist. "I was so worried about the both of you."

Adam starts to pull away, but Cy clings to him for just another second. Then he steps back as Allure lowers Cy to the ground with the lift.

Michael and Adam both drop to their knees on either side of her chair, and for a moment, they all hold each other, tears flowing, even from Mane and Allure, who quietly watch the homecoming from the top of the ramp by the door.

As Cy holds her boys, Michael feels strong and controlled, almost too controlled, while in her other arm, Adam's entire body is trembling. Cy knows that her sons are going to handle this loss in their own ways and that neither of their paths will be easy.

After a moment, they let go of one another, and Michael pushes her up the ramp. Adam right behind them.

"Where's Wizard?" Cy asks, looking around. "Is he OK?"

"He's fine, waiting in the kitchen," Adam answers.

"Sorry we could only score you a manual-use, fold-up wheelchair," offers Allure. "That's all we had access to."

"Good for my upper body anyway," Cy responds. "But if I'm going to get through this, I need to drive my own chair. Michael, can you hand me control please?"

At the top of the ramp, Michael relinquishes control and Cy pushes her way into the lean-to, where she notices something else missing.

"And where's R3x?" she asks.

Adam and Michael look at each other, and Michael answers first.

"R3x is in the workroom. We're just finishing up the final touches on the hot lasers," he says.

"Wow. You've been busy," she responds.

"Yeah. He's ready to shoot lasers from his butt and his eyes," Adam adds. "We just need to test him."

"Well … I'd like to be around when you conduct *that* test," she responds.

Because she's in a wheelchair, Cy takes the dumbwaiter to the ground floor while the rest of the group uses the staircase. As she descends, she closes her eyes and savors the smell of something delicious cooking in the kitchen.

"Let me guess. Wild turkey and rice?" she asks. "I take it the cooking is Michael's work?"

"Yes, well, both of us really," answers Michael as he emerges from the staircase. "We knew you'd be hungry for fresh nutritious food, as you like to call it. So, Adam gathered, and I hunted."

"It looks like you thought of everything," Cy says, pausing a moment to appreciate her sons yet again.

Wizard, still in an apron from setting up their meal, steps out to greet her.

"Hello, mistress," he says, trying to be cheery but not doing a very good job of it. "We have missed your presence around here."

He looks drawn and older than the last time she saw him—which was only a week ago.

"Hello, Wizard. Thanks for being here for my sons, for us all," Cy responds.

As their eyes mist up again, Allure changes the subject.

"Wizard, what's the plan for Cy's PT?" Allure asks. "When we left, Med!c said he'd handle it, but he's not here."

"Med!c came and went already," Wizard answers. "Oh, and he wants his ambulance back now that you've used it to transport Cy back to us, which means he won't be gone too long."

Then turning to Cy directly, he adds, "He left an exercise and hydrotherapy plan to strengthen your arms, shoulders, and core."

"We've all had training on moving your legs and feet for you, as well as helping you into and out of the bed and stuff," Adam adds helpfully.

Cy closes her eyes, trying not to think of herself as weak and needing assistance to do these very basic things, but it's not working.

"Um, and I'm here to help get you through your personal routine and into bed for the next few days until we learn ways you can handle it yourself," Allure offers. "I mean, if you don't mind."

Cy cringes at the thought of being so needy.

"Ugh, I wish everyone would stop talking about my helplessness," she complains, her eyes still closed.

"Of course. Apologies, mistress," Wizard responds. "But your boys, and all of us, we're just trying to help, and we're working to enable you to actually be independent again."

Cy realizes she sounds like a dick. "I'm sorry, boys. And thank you for all that you are doing, my thanks to all of you," she offers.

Just then, Cy's stomach rumbles loudly. Wizard hands her a bowl of soup and sets a cup of water down on a short table adjacent to the kitchen counter that they'd tailored to her chair.

"The kitchen was harder to adjust since the counters are all carved in stone. So, the boys put a movable worktable over here for you that a wheelchair can fit under," Wizard explains.

They all eat in silence, trying not to look at Cy as she awkwardly picks up her spoon and tries to navigate eating from a wheelchair with no control over her lower body.

"Don't forget to eat slowly," Allure offers. "Your stomach's been empty a long time."

Cy manages to get a half bowl of soup down, mostly the broth, one spoon at a time. When she's done, Wizard suggests the boys show her around.

"The rest of us can just hang back here with the soup," adds Mane as he pours a second bowl for Allure and himself.

The boys take her to the workroom where Cy almost feels herself again. She sees R3x on a workbench near the door and then notices two modified worktables to fit her wheelchair.

"Some of the tabletops now include levers to raise, lower, or move side to side," Adam offers, showing her. "Here, like this."

Cy pulls up to the table and takes the lever from him, turning it to adjust the table surface to fit just above the arms on her chair.

"This works! Thank you," she says with appreciation. "Hopefully, I won't be needing this for too long."

"There's more," Michael says. "We did some modifications to the bathroom."

The doors into all the rooms are, thankfully, wide enough for her chair to fit through without issue. In the bathroom, the toilet has been raised with arms to the side so she can transfer herself more easily. There's also a new lift next to the tub.

"We're still trying to figure out how to give you easier sink access. Maybe something like a short hose?" says Michael, trying to be helpful.

"I think I can pull up to the tub and just use the removable shower head, can't I?" Cy surmises. "If we can keep that within my reach—"

"We also put an arm rail on your bed in your room," Adam

interrupts excitedly. "We couldn't get a hospital bed. So hopefully, this will work."

Cy looks in her room and freezes as the moments she last shared with Des come flooding back. She feels him there, on their big bed, the bearskin rug …

> A week ago, Cy was brushing her hair at her antique dressing table, facing a large round mirror in the candlelit bedroom. Des, shirtless and trim with a solid six-pack, watched her in the mirror as he stood behind her. He took the brush from her and continued brushing her hair for her. After a minute, he set it down and dropped the strap of her cami, bending to kiss her shoulder, her neck.
>
> She turned to him, looking up into his hazel eyes, touching his hips, running her hands along his six-pack, kissing his belly. Then he pulled her up to her feet, cradling her face and looking her in the eye as if, possibly, for the last time. He kissed her deeply, and they dropped to the bearskin rug …

Cy is frozen there, looking in her room that's empty and strange without Des. She doesn't even realize she's speaking when she asks, "How can things have changed so much so fast?"

Adam and Michael have no answer, so they all return to the kitchen in silence.

"We aren't the only ones suffering losses, you know," Cy says to all of them. "The whole world is in chaos because of what we did. I never wanted guns, kamikaze drones, and lasers. But I was outnumbered by the rest of the clan leaders."

"Dad loved that about you, Mom—your aversion to violence," Michael remembers fondly. "Yet you could defeather a wild turkey or skin and dress a deer or wild boar, no problem."

"That's for food—for sustenance of family and crew," Cy answers. *"It's not the same."*

Adam takes this moment to ask the question that's been burning in him since Wizard gave him the news his parents had been shot.

"Mom, I have to know. How did you get shot by GlobeCom's drone?" he asks. "Weren't you using the drone-signal blockers Michael and I designed with Dad? Did they fail? Is it *our* fault?"

He runs a hand through his messy hair and then continues. "I mean, we thought of *everything,* so how could this happen to you? To Dad?"

Cy rolls her chair to Adam and puts a hand on his arm, attempting to calm him.

"How did the drone shot get through? I don't know, actually," Cy answers honestly. "We were using the signal blockers, and they were definitely disabling GlobeCom drones during the entire operation. Then we ran to the truck. Last thing I remember is Allure firing the EMP."

Cy looks at Allure for an answer.

Allure moves away from the counter and looks at all of them.

"The signal blockers worked perfectly. But we'd all turned off our electronics and put them in the Faraday bags at the time Cy was shot. It … That last drone came around a corner and in range just after I had fired the initial pulse. The damn GlobeCom drone got in one round before I could fire again. That's what hit your parents," she explains, her eyes tearing up. "Sorry … so sorry."

Mane, who'd been trying to sound sympathetic this whole time, finally loses his grace. He can't handle everyone feeling sorry for themselves.

"It's not your fault, my darling Allure. It's not Adam's fault or Michael's fault either, so don't blame yourselves. Guilt is a useless emotion," Mane interjects impatiently. "Your drone disruptors worked as they were supposed to, boys. It was just the perfect storm. An alignment of happenstances that led to a millisecond of exposure when that drone blasted through."

SEVENTEEN YEARS EARLIER

Cy's security detail arrived at zero nine hundred on a Tuesday morning in late June. She was setting in tomatoes, peppers, and other heat- and sun-loving produce in the hottest spot of her fenced-in garden. R3x stood near her, recharging his batteries in a sunny spot. A shiny black rat snake slithered through the fencing, making Cy shudder, even though Wizard educated her on how black snakes are good snakes because they actually do eat rats and other pesky rodents that are after her garden. It was the timber rattlers he told her to look out for, which they keep antivenom for in the fridge.

Cy stood and wiped her muddy hands on her work apron, hoping her new bodyguard was all d_ArkAngl made him out to be. More importantly, she hoped he would be easy to get along with—since he'd be sleeping in the room across the hall from hers. She wasn't worried about his military background because she understood that mindset, but the unknown worried her. And she hated that she needed protection in the first place, even though she knew that, in these backwoods, she couldn't live alone—even with Wizard less than a quarter mile from her.

Once Wizard parked his truck next to the garage, Cy's new bodyguard, a little too eager, bounded out and hurried toward her—that is until R3x barked at him, stopping him in his tracks about four feet away.

The pause gave her a chance to check him out: tall, chiseled, well-chested with sun-kissed sandy-blond hair—almost a Ken doll, but a military version.

He looked up at Cy curiously. She laughed lightly at his confusion about R3x and then explained what the dog was doing.

"R3x, my robot dog here, is asking for you to authenticate through voice command," she said. "First, you need to make up a passcode you can remember because you will use it each time you get called out by R3x."

Des looked at her quizzically and then back at R3x, thinking. R3x barked again, and Des stepped forward.

"I do solemnly swear that I will support and defend the Constitution of the United States against all enemies, foreign and domestic," he said with a light Midwestern accent.

Cy approved his passcode, and R3x stopped barking to process. After a second, R3x looked up at him with his blank camera eyes and wagged his little robot tail.

"So, I assume I'm authenticated!" he observed.

He was formal, sincere, and disarming all at the same time. She nodded affirmatively as he reached out his hand.

"Nice to meet you, CyAnthia, ma'am," Des said, shaking her hand heartily. "I'm Des0l8tion, but you can call me Des for short."

"Hello, Des, nice to meet you. And you can call me Cy," she answered.

Her handshake left his palm with a light layer of orangish dirt. He tried to wipe it off with his other hand, which just made it spread.

"Sorry about that. I was gardening. Mud and dirt: impossible to avoid and spreads everywhere ... like the snakes," she explained.

Des caught the humor and smiled broadly as he detected a black rat snake slithering into a hollow in a nearby tree.

"It's OK, ma'am. I've lived in jungles where the snakes are bigger than I am," he answered. "And some snakes make good food."

Cy was quickly lost in his looks, wondering why d_ArkAngl would send her such a fine specimen of a man, especially while her hormones were raging.

"Are you from Nebraska?" she asked, trying to sound casual.

"Thereabouts. I'm guessing you picked it out in my accent?" he answered.

Before she could respond, Wizard caught up with them.

"Oh good. Glad to see you two getting on," he said, handing Cy a case of peaches. "Here are the stone fruits you requested. There are more in the car—like you asked for your canning."

Cy buried her face in the box, inhaling the aroma.

"Thank you for remembering, Wizard! They smell so good," she said.

"Seeds are fertile, so you can start your little fruit orchard with the pits, just as your heart desires, mistress," Wizard explained.

"Wonderful! And, of course, you get some of the jams. And the cobbler," she said, taking another whiff of the aromatic peaches.

"Thank you for your kindness, mistress," Wizard said. "I remain forever your servant."

She looked at Des and winked. "Wizard doesn't know how to cook, so he charms me into feeding him," she confided. "But he is learning how to tend chickens, so he'll repay in eggs soon ... Do you cook?"

"Yes, ma'am. I can prep and cook mostly wild game," Des answered.

"That's good," Cy noted. "And I could use some hunting and fishing lessons. Do you fish? We've already figured out crawdads—easy to catch on strings and taste like lobster ..."

"Mm one of my favorites, creek lobsters with salted butter," Wizard responded, smiling at the thought. "Now let's go inside and show you around a bit."

"Inside where?" Des asked. "I don't see anything."

"Exactly!" said Wizard, slapping his thigh and laughing. "That's what they *all* say the first time."

Over the next three months, Des and Cy had become close room-mates, so much so that they decided it was best to perpetuate the story that the baby she carried was his. This, they decided, would protect d_ArkAngl and the rest of their growing clan if any of them were caught.

Cy was in that awkward large stage of the pregnancy where she felt like a duck. Tonight, she dressed regally in off-white robes and looked more like a Madonna prepared to meet her royal subjects.

Upon arrival, their new members all submitted to Des scanning their persons, vehicles, carry bags, and equipment for any technologies emitting signals that could be traced. Once satisfied they were not emitting such signals, he escorted them to the hide-out where they were met by Cy and R3x.

The first guest, Allure, twenty-nine, stood six feet tall without shoes and weighed a scant 130 pounds. She enhanced her thin, ghoulish figure by wearing a skintight, sleeveless unitard and six-inch stilettos. Yet, despite the heels, she managed to gracefully squat down and pet R3x affectionately.

"Cool, a little robot doggie—but in a creepy, blank-stare kind of way," she said.

R3x looked up at her expectantly with its camera eyes and barked.

"Oh, how delightful! Is he asking me to authenticate?" she asked.

"Actually, yes," Cy answered.

Once entered into the R3x system, their three new arrivals were taken downstairs, while R3x maintained his post upstairs. Their guests were greeted with the wonderful aroma of wild blackberry cobbler, still warm from the oven, which Cy had set out on the counter between the kitchen and the roundtable, along with coffee and tea service.

"Please help yourselves," Cy offered as their new clan members looked at the food hungrily.

Without hesitation, they all filled their plates with firsts and then seconds.

Des waited for everyone to settle at the table before beginning the official meeting of the blue ridge mountain clan.

"How many of you can get the food you need without a UI?" he asked them. "Are there any stores within an hour of here that will let you shop without one?"

They all paused, looking around at one another. Bilbo, twenty-three, wiped a berry from the side of his mouth.

"We find places to get food with cloned plastic, yes, but not many," Bilbo answered. About five foot five and slightly portly with large, hairy bare feet, Bilbo actually looked like the hobbit from J. R. R. Tolkien's *Lord of the Rings* trilogy. Hacker legend had it that, just like in the trilogy, this Bilbo never wore shoes, even in the winter.

"Mostly we can get food from roadside stands that are not outfitted with UI readers yet," Bilbo continued. "Probably in a year, we won't even have those options."

Allure, with a deep, sultry voice, offered an idea. "Some of us have been thinking of dumpster diving. I mean, we're not too far from the Homestead Hot Springs Resort, and they feed people there all day long, don't they?"

Cy wrinkled her nose in distaste. "Hopefully, it won't come to dumpster diving," she responded. "Des and I have something that might help us shop and eat like everyone else."

On cue, Des placed what looked like a clear bandage on the table in front of Cy to pass around. She held it up to the light to show it had tiny, embedded circuits that looked like Braille.

"These things make the scanners and the readers go crazy and do your bidding," Des said, explaining the technology. "You stick it on the back of your wrist like a bandage and then waive it at the barcode reader. You walk out with your food, and the merchant system is none the wiser."

"The tape self-destructs the moment you leave the premise. It becomes completely useless and forensically unrecoverable, so it cannot be used to reverse engineer our technology or track back to us," Cy added.

She passed the tape to Mane, a large, barrel-chested fellow on her right. Mane, thirty-one, with a light Bronx accent, wore a brocaded vest of olden days and carried a carved wooden cane with a bronze lion's head handle.

Cy noticed Allure eyeing Mane and smiled slightly at the image of how the two of them would look together.

"Right. I see you've thought of everything but for one little point," said Mane, pouring liquor from a silver flask into his coffee. "You know ... The feds are elevating first-time hacking to a capital crime with up to fifteen years in work camp. That little thing. They're even talking about the death penalty."

No one answered as he looked around the table at each of them.

"So, my question is: do we even want to do this?" he continued.

Cy sighed and shook her head in acknowledgement. "Yes, *that*. And things will likely get worse," she agreed. "Do any of you want to bail? If so, now's the time ..."

"Believe me, I've already thought of it," Mane said as he stole a look at Allure. "But I'm going to stick around awhile and see how things go."

Allure looked back at Mane, raising a penciled eyebrow questioningly.

"OK, so we're all here of our own accord. That's good," Des said, steering the conversation back on track. "There's no doubt we're all gifted technologists. But up here, we get by with what we can build, buy, grow, hunt, barter, trade, or steal. So, we need to take inventory of everyone's survival skills."

Wizard pulled a joint from his pocket and lit it. "Well, I have one skill, and it's medicinal if anyone needs it," he said half joking but also serious. "I heard it's also good for labor pain."

Cy rolled her eyes as if she'd been through this before.

"That smells good," said Bilbo as the sweet smoke wafted his way. "Mind if I have a toke?"

As Wizard passed the joint, Cy continued.

"I spent six years with a foster family on a corn farm an hour away from the nearest grocery, so I can grow, harvest, butcher, and cook just about anything," Cy said. Then, rubbing her growing baby bump, she added, "We're hoping one of you can help us deliver this baby."

To that, Allure raised her hand sheepishly. "I might be able to help. I've assisted two midwifery births," she offered. "And as for other survival skills, I am also good with guns. I'm fond of automatics, especially AKs."

To that, Mane looked at the alien-like Allure with even more interest.

"Mane, what's your specialty?" Cy asked.

"Specialties—plural," Mane said, a little full of himself. "First, I'm a generalist: I can write code and break code just as easily. Second, I know how to outfit the Wi-Fi towers to support our local network, so as to make our presence here undetectable to fly-by surveillance."

"Excellent! You need to work with Wizard on that," Cy noted.

"I'm also good at hacking drone signals," Mane added, "if that can be of any use."

"Drones are my thing," Des responded excitedly. "I'm working on some signal channel blockers of my own."

"You show me yours; I'll show you mine," Mane offered. "Lead the way."

"How about a tour of our workroom?" Des suggested to everyone. "Bring your gear. We have enough space for all of you."

Inside the workroom, Bilbo looked around and then selected his worktable in the middle.

"This should do nicely," Bilbo said as he opened his pack and spread out his chip cloning tools on it.

"Those cloning tools look similar to the tools used to make fake credit cards," Cy observed.

"Yeah, very similar. But these will carry far more information than just banking chip data," Bilbo answered. "And the data on the chips can be tailored. For example, what if Cy needed treatment for type 1 diabetes? She must have a matching identity, blood type, and similar medical history to get the proper care when she needs it. Think of it. We can clone partial or entire identities for our own critical needs as they arise."

"Very intriguing," said Des, impressed. "How do you collect the right medical data and align it with, say, my blood type?"

"I've been testing walk-by scanning of other people's UIs," Bilbo answered, eager to share. "I've got loads of data, but we need a database to sort it so that we can tailor the chips for each of us."

"Smart!" said Cy, who then felt suddenly disappointed. "Except that I find it ironic that we're committing the same type of identity crimes that I used to uncover in my prior life."

"So, we commit identity theft. We do so responsibly and out of necessity," responded Wizard, now fully baked. "Today's laws—they don't apply to us because we no longer exist. And today's law is GlobeCom law. Fuck today's law because justice is fucked."

Wizard's words gave Mane an idea.

"That's it! I think you just named our clan," Mane said. "How about we call ourselves UnFucking Justice—UFJ for short. You know, now that justice is fucked, we have to unfuck it."

Des, chuckling, put it up to vote.

"That's a great idea! All in favor?" he asked.

In unison, they all said, "Aye!"

CHAPTER 7.

DESOL8TION RIDGE

PRESENT DAY

The sun descends behind the western mountains, painting ridge after ridge in a midnight blue hue. At the top of one of these ridges, two dozen hackers and leaders from UFJ and nearby clans fidget in fold-up camp chairs, waiting for Cy to speak. They'd come in contingents, with leaders from six separate clans here to pay their respects.

Cy sits in her wheelchair at the head of her husband's grave, her black lace veil swaying lightly in the mountain winds. Adam and Michael, also dressed in black, are positioned on either side of her. Her boys had planted a new azalea on the center of the grave (over the heart) that should burst into vibrant red blooms next spring—the color of the ultimate sacrifice but also of new blood and rebirth. Before the ceremony, Cy (with the help of Allure) had also placed a colorful spray of asters and yellow daisies at the head of the grave.

Pri3st, sixty-five, stands near the bereaved family, Bible in hand. Dressed in an off-white robe with colorful embroidery around the cuffs and neck, he is tall and slender with short-cropped white hair and shiny black skin. Pri3st is a pastor to the off-grid community with a booming voice and message of hope and resurrection for the just.

After a few moments of silently looking at the view of the ridges, Cy straightens, shoulders back, chin high, and turns her chair to face the audience.

"This is where Des used to sit for hours and stare at the mountain peaks beyond," she tells them. "He could be spitting mad when he left for this ridge. But no matter what was vexing him, he would always come back with a solution. Or a boar. Once, it was a bear. And most times, he'd come back whistling."

Just then, a gust of wind sweeps through the canyons that sounds like a whistle. Adam and Michael each take one of Cy's hands in theirs. After another moment of silence, Cy raises her sons' hands with hers over her head and claims this spot for Des.

"In honor of our fallen soldier, we will now call this place Des0l8tion Ridge," she proclaims.

To that, everyone but Cy stands. Then they spontaneously chant together, "Des0l8tion Ridge! Des0l8tion Ridge! Des0l8tion Ridge!" while pitching their right fists into the air.

Once they all take their seats again, Pri3st steps forward to start the invocation. "We are here to celebrate the man, the soldier, the husband, and the freedom fighter who was Des0l8tion," he says in a deep Southern voice that echoes through the canyons. "We are here to remember a man who loved country and family above himself. He was a unifier, strategist, and skilled technologist. And despite all that he had going for him, he was humble. Having known him for these past fifteen years, I also believe he was a God-fearing man because he would give you the shirt off his back and brought us many needed supplies for survival."

Everyone nods and gestures their agreement.

"As generous as he was, Des was not a man to be trifled with. He exacted the same type of loyalty that he gave to each of us," Pri3st adds.

Several in the audience nod again in acknowledgement.

"I remember once, Des and his bonnie wife, Cy, here, were feeding us venison tacos, all nice and cozy until Des found a signal emitting from my wrist set," says Skew, who's wearing his best kilt for the occasion. "Then he comes up behind me fast and sudden, his wand scanning me all over the place. I could *see* those biceps bulging very close to my face and wondered if I was going to *die*."

Skew pauses as everyone has a knowing chuckle. They all recognize him as the leader from the north Virginia arm of Cl0ver Clan that originated in Dublin. The Irish clans were critical in taking out GlobeCom's ICHEC (Irish Centre for High-End Computing) centers during Operation Backbone.

"Oh yeah, I was scared as piss all right … at least until Des realized it was a short-range signal emitter in my pocket, and I told him we used the emitters to find other people's chips, decrypt them, and collect the data from them," Skew continues. "Right away, my man Des switched from intimidating to curious, all light and cool as if he'd never been up in my face. And then he starts asking about all kinds of uses for the scanners beyond what we built them for."

Everyone shares another knowing look.

"Some will never know the sacrifices made by our brave cyberwarriors," Cy says, pausing to look at each one of them. "But this loss is not in vain. We are seeing the shift of power back to individual humans who are piecing together their own data histories even now. Let's not forget that Des would want us to complete the plan, protect the people during this chaotic transition, and help them build a more transparent system that works for the benefit everyone, not just the pigs at GlobeCom who've been helping themselves to the trough."

Everyone expresses their agreement, some even standing again as they do so. Adam and Michael, meanwhile, seem transfixed by Skew's daughter, sixteen-year-old Saoirse (pronounced *Seersha*, which means freedom). Her eyes are still the piercing green they always were, even with her signature black eyeliner washed away. Petite and curvy, her shiny auburn hair is worn straight and long to her waist.

Adam, trying not to stare, suffers a mix of emotions—most of which he can barely understand let alone keep up with. Cy senses Adam's discomfort and places a hand gently on his knee. Michael, meanwhile, is worried that Saoirse might be up to her old tricks. Since they were children, she loved playing the two brothers against each other. He's pretty sure that this last time, though, it was *he* who screwed up and drove her away. He's just not sure what he *did*.

As the boys ruminate, Med!c rises to continue the remembrance of Des, the man, the soldier, and the protector of the clans.

"I was with our Des as he died. To the very end, he did not want to let go of Cy's hand," he says thoughtfully.

Cy quietly sobs, and Med!c moves to a better memory.

"Mostly, I remember his drones … how Des used them to sneak up on you by flying low and slow through the woods without ever hitting anything he didn't want to hit. Crazy-accurate driving," he continues. "But you know, especially in the winter, his drones came in handy for deliveries and saved us having to go out in the cold to share kale and potatoes or medical supplies. So, it's the practical stuff like that I think I'll miss most."

Allure, in a black bodysuit, stands next and shares her memories.

"I was honored to be with Des in his life—and his death,"

says Allure, trying not to cry. "He taught me to fight, and he was relentless in his training, just like he was with his pursuit of freedom."

Next, Mane speaks but without rising. His heavy weight and the soft, uneven ground aren't good odds for standing up from his teetering camp chair without falling. Today he wears black pants and a gold vest with no shirt, and he has with him his signature lion head cane.

"I'm with Med!c on the drones," Mane says after Allure sits back down beside him. "He loved using drones to blow things up—with his own home-made explosives, no less. These skills and his technical knowledge were critical in defeating the GlobeCom drones."

As if on cue, Adam and Michael stand in unison, while Skew reaches down for his bagpipe. Skew starts playing "Taps," while Adam and Michael use their controllers to direct two drones over the grave and unfurl an American flag between them. Everyone (but Cy and Mane) stands respectfully with hands over their hearts as the flag hovers in place above the grave through the full rendition of "Taps."

"We couldn't give Dad the twenty-one-gun salute that he deserves without waking up the neighbors," Michael tells everyone once the music ends. "So instead, Adam and I thought this would honor him just as well."

Pri3st points to the boys with an expression of great pride on his face. "This act right here—this combination of thoughtfulness, planning, and execution—this is a testament to how well Des raised two young men to carry on for him," Pri3st proclaims. "Two young men with their own skills and fresh minds who will help us rebuild a system where no one controls us."

To this, Cy silently blanches but says nothing. Pri3st and Wizard, even Des, have been telling her that the boys are ready for prime time, and she knows they are right, but she's afraid of losing them to a work camp or worse.

Adam and Michael call back their drones, roll up the flag, and pack them into their carrying cases. Then Cy thanks everyone and directs them to the food table filled with potluck from the visiting clans.

Skew and Elven light a preset bonfire and setup for making s'mores, which were among Des's favorite treats. Michael watches them, particularly Elven, who's a colorful cross between his Irish father and his South African mother (who died in childbirth). Elven is dressed stylishly (as usual) in tight black satin slacks and a formfitting silver and black-threaded tank.

Michael takes his leave of Adam to talk with Elven, and Saoirse meets up with Adam near the bonfire. She looks at him in the firelight. She's vulnerable and still teary-eyed. Adam hands her a handkerchief. She blows her nose in it, making a little honking sound, and then tries to give it back.

"Keep it," Adam says. "It was a gift from Dad. I have a whole pack of them."

"Thank you. I needed something to remember him by," Saoirse responds. "And I wanted to say ... I ... I'm just so sorry for your loss."

To that, Adam looks down, conflicted. Finally, he mumbles down to his feet. "I don't know what to say to that. I ... I didn't really think you cared that much. I mean, you've been gone a whole year."

Saoirse looks more crushed than she already did. "How could you even *say* that?" she demands angrily. "Des was like an uncle to me, and you know it! I've avoided you because you were a total ass that night, and you never apologized. And if you hadn't noticed, you never looked me up during all that time either ..."

Before Adam can reply, Michael returns and butts in. "Guys! Guys! Something interesting is happening over at the food table," he says excitedly. "The adults are arguing about something important."

Like when they were children, Michael, Adam, and Saoirse make their way over to food table area and then hang back quietly in the shadows to eavesdrop on the spirited discussion going on among their elders.

Wizard, now nearing his seventieth birthday, is speaking about next steps. "GlobeCom will be sending their goons after us," he assesses. "We've crippled their ability to organize rapid response, but they still have pull over the military—not to mention their private security."

"Yeah, so we've been thinking about that in the Cl0 clans," Skew answers, his Irish accent more pronounced than usual tonight. "Now is the time to hit their last stronghold—their security forces. And we should start with their chief security officers."

At the mention of the GlobeCom CSOs, Cy is suddenly alarmed about d_ArkAngl. Oblivious to her reaction, Skew continues.

"They all hang out in the same social forums, so we've already got their profiles and shared intel," he continues. "For example, the China CSO, Leonard Smith—he's fond of staying at the Watergate Hotel, close to the GlobeCom DC hub, where they have another CSO, Ron Meeker. We were thinking one stone, two birds if we can find them in the same location."

Wizard goes pale at the mention of Leonard Smith, while Cy can barely hold back from screaming at the top of her lungs to stop them. All this time, d_ArkAngl's real identity of Leonard Smith as CSO of GlobeCom's China hub is known to nobody but Cy and Wizard. This is for everyone's safety, or else her whole clan would be at risk—her children, Des, everyone. Not to mention the risk to d_ArkAngl, who's embedded in a country where they make deadly examples of their digital enemies.

The group before him has no idea that the legendary d_ArkAngl is actually Leonard Smith who's been squirreling out GlobeCom logistics, signal channels and crypto algorithms, security technologies and prototypes, drones, and more to give the clans the advantage.

Cy is panicking internally while trying to maintain calm on the outside. She looks around at each of them, wondering what to do. They all seem to be waiting on her to respond.

"Is that really necessary?" she finally asks. "Going after the CSOs, who are obviously just doing their jobs defending their company networks like any of us would do if we were in their shoes?"

For a moment, everyone is quiet and considering her words, all of them aware of her aversion to violence. Looking at Cy gives them more pause than normal. She's their inspiration in this fight that wound up putting her in this wheelchair—and her husband in the grave next to her.

Mane finally breaks the silence. "Yeah, but see we're not doing their jobs, are we? No, we're not," he says sardonically. "Even though we're qualified and more talented than they are, we chose not to put our skills to work for the dark side."

"We aren't violent people!" Cy objects, sounding a little desperate.

The three teens hiding in the shadows look at each other and share concerned expressions.

"We don't plan on hurting anybody, just get their access creds," Skew clarifies. "Most likely, we can do that by scanning their chips up close and stealing their biometrics."

Cy tries another tactic. "Phase two was to social engineer around the power vacuum, set the GlobeCom twenty-four board members against each other, and steer them back into their old cold war ways of killing each other," she reminds them. "We must focus on that first."

"Well, from what we hear, that's already happening," Skew responds, while others in the group nod their heads as if they'd heard the same news. "But we still need CSO-level access to move things along."

At this point, everyone starts talking at once, sharing ideas on how to execute the plan. They are so engrossed in plotting their next move that nobody (but for the teens quietly watching them) notices as Cy and Wizard quietly slip away into the night.

SEVENTEEN YEARS EARLIER—TIES THAT BIND

Cy floated in her deep, heart-shaped granite tub, the warm water comforting her through the pain. With each contraction, her belly hardened like a watermelon above the water, while her nails dug into Des's arm. Even as she made him bleed, he sat stoically on the cool stone floor beside the tub, continuing to lend her his hand over the side of the tub.

"Come on, girl. You can do this," coached Allure as she kneeled in the water, facing Cy's bent legs.

"Shit, hell, fuck! Why do you have to *do that* in the middle of contraction?" Cy screamed.

"Breathe, baby, breathe," said Allure as she continued to check where the cresting head was. "Do it like we practiced. You're fully dilated now, the head is here, and everything is in order."

Twenty-three miles away at the Homestead Resort, d_ArkAngl paced his large, plantation-style suite at the Homestead Hot Springs Resort. He used this location primarily for its low-tech, deep-south, meandering grounds. There were very few cameras here, and the entire property was a no-fly zone on account of people undressing to get into the pools and paying richly for the right to do so without being watched.

Finally, d_ArkAngl's messenger lit up and he stopped his pacing to read the purposefully cryptic communication sent over local cell towers to his wristband.

"Sonny Skies, all is well," the message read before deleting itself.

d_ArkAngl noted the misspelled word for sunny and smiled reflectively, his glasses misting up.

"I have a son!" he said aloud. "A healthy baby boy!"

Within minutes, d_ArkAngl was on the road driving toward Cy, a loaded picnic basket on the seat beside him. The drive took an excruciating sixty minutes, half of it off-road on their hidden property. When he finally arrived at Cy's sod-covered garage, Wizard was waiting eagerly for him out front, just as he had on the day he waited to meet Cy for the first time. As d_ArkAngl stepped out of the car, Wizard pulled him into a bearhug.

"So good to see you, my boy. So good to see you," said Wizard, who already looked like a true mountain man with a grisly beard and long graying hair.

"You too, old man. You too," replied d_ArkAngl, patting Wizard lightly.

They pulled apart and examined each other. Wizard wore a white long-sleeved tunic-style cotton shirt with leather lacing at the neck.

"I dig the moccasins. What are they, deerskin?" d_ArkAngl asked, looking down at Wizard's feet.

"Yes. Des made them. I'm just breaking them in," Wizard rambled. "They're remarkably warm and waterproof—something about the tanning process."

d_ArkAngl looked conflicted, so Wizard wisely switched the topic away from the other man in Cy's life.

"Anyhow, you're looking healthy," Wizard said, quickly pivoting. "Someone in Beijing must be feeding you."

"Yes. Long story, and I need to do the courtesy of informing Cy about it first," d_ArkAngl answered. "How is she?"

"Mother and baby are fine," Wizard informed him. "They're in their room, resting. Allure is back at her cabin with Mane, and Des is at my place. You have until nine tonight before they return."

"That's almost twelve hours give or take," acknowledged d_ ArkAngl. "Not a lot of time but at least something."

"If anything happens and you need us, reach me over our local network. Cy knows the codes," Wizard offered.

A few minutes later, after authenticating past R3x, d_ ArkAngl found Cy on her side in a large feather bed, her back to the door. She was half asleep, nursing a swaddled pink baby with a light fluff of strawberry blond hair. He put down his things and climbed into the bed behind her, spooning her and looking over her shoulder at the baby nursing on her full breast.

"Hello, my love. You have never been as beautiful or as magical as you are now," he said adoringly.

Cy turned her head halfway to meet his gaze, smiling lovingly. "Hello, my darling," she said before turning back to her infant. "We did it. He's eight pounds, strong, and healthy with all his fingers and toes. And he's smart. He knew how to nurse straight out of the canal."

"Ah, my mini-me! Loves breasts like I do," he said with a light lecherous chuckle. "May I hold him?"

"I dunno. Are your hands clean?" she asked. "After all, he is a little newborn baby, not exposed to germs and pathogens just yet, and I'd like to keep it that way for a little while."

Lightly amused by her maternal instinct, d_ArkAngl deferred playfully, saying, "Yes, mistress. It was a long drive, and I need to take a leak anyway."

He returned, refreshed and clean, and Cy handed over the baby.

"Here you go. He just finished nursing. Let me show you how to burp him," she offered.

"I think I know how," he said, propping the eight-pound bundle on his chest and lightly rubbing and patting his lower back. "Like this, right?"

Cy nodded affirmatively, and he continued.

"I'd like to name him Adam. For new beginnings. Our first

baby ... and born truly off-grid ... no digital record of any kind," d_ArkAngl said thoughtfully.

"Adam. No last name. I like that," Cy responded.

Adam burped loudly, as if he approved, and they both laughed. Then Adam snuggled into his father's chest and fell fast asleep. d_ArkAngl was instantly enraptured. His heart had never felt so full as in this moment or so tender as it did for the little human in his arms.

As he continued to cradle the baby against his chest, he examined Cy's room. The adjustable lighting felt like morning at this moment, reflecting off the curved walls of gray and black granite, polished of sharp edges. There were two mirrored oak armoires wedged in nooks in the rock. Between them was an antique 1940s-style vanity table with large round mirror.

"Love what you and Wizard have done with the place," he observed.

"It *is* beautiful, thanks mostly to what you'd already had done before I got here," she answered. "Also, Wizard turns out to be a hell of a garage-sale buddy."

With his free hand, d_ArkAngl reached down into the picnic basket, pulled out a Tiffany case, and handed it to Cy.

"This is just a very small token of my appreciation for having our child—out here in the backwoods, no less," he said. "You are truly amazing. So, hopefully this little gift will remind you of how much I love you for being the badass that you are."

Cy opened the velvet box to see a perfect strand of large-gauge black pearls.

"These pearls. They're ...they're ... breathtaking. I mean, look at the luminescence," she responded. "Thank you, thank you, my love. But ... Where would I possibly wear them?"

"Wear them here. Wear them now. Wear them to Adam's milestone moments in life. Or yours," he said. "And if you need them for trade or money, you use them for that."

She put the necklace on and felt the weight and coolness of the pearls on her skin.

"Beautiful," he said, lightly touching them with his free hand. "When you're fully recovered, I'd love to see you wearing nothing but those pearls with stockings and heels."

"You're incorrigible," she responded teasingly. "That's actually the *last* thing on my mind right now."

Cy's stomach rumbled, so d_ArkAngl handed the sleeping Adam back to her, and she laid him on his side in his bassinette by her side of the bed. d_ArkAngl put the picnic basket in Cy's lap and opened it. Her eyes widened as she went through the contents: cheeses, nut butters, lunchmeats, fresh fruits, dark chocolates, her favorite Kona coffee beans, sourdough starter, and so much more.

"It feels like Christmas from around the world … but in October," Cy said as she poured over the culinary treasures.

The little family of three spent a luxurious day together, eating, cuddling, sleeping, feeding, and changing the baby—repeat. For one day, they felt like a new family and savored this time together because they knew it was fleeting.

Finally, as d_ArkAngl prepared to take his leave, he broached a subject he'd been dreading to bring up. "We have to talk about something that will make you sad," he said gently as he held her in his arms. "I'm sorry for the timing on this … but I just don't know when I'll see you again, and we need to talk about this in person, face-to-face."

She sat up so she could see his face. "Sounds ominous."

"Please try not to make me bleed like you did to Des," he teased lightly as he fluffed some pillows behind her to support her back.

"Not … responsible … for what I do when in the throes of hard labor," she teased back.

Then they grew serious again.

"It's about my cover in Beijing," d_ArkAngl explained. "It

looks odd, a man in his prime, great job, good financial situation, with *no* significant other … People are asking why I'm not matched up."

Her heart dropped as she realized where this was going, but she said nothing, waiting for him to explain.

"If I'm to survive this, I've got to make a convincing cover of the hardworking family man in Beijing," he said before pausing to clear his throat. "I'm … I'm being pressured to take a wife."

Cy, not normally a jealous person, felt an enormous pang of envy for whoever this other woman was. Someone else would get to live and be seen with *her* man when she was stranded far away.

"Who is she? Is she Chinese or American? Is she beautiful?" Cy asked.

"Do you really want to know?"

"Yes, I want to know," she responded. "That's why I'm asking."

"Her name is Ying Liu. She is first daughter of China hub's board director, esteemed mother, Nǚ Jiāzhǎng," he said apologetically. "It feels prearranged, I think partly to keep an eye on me."

Cy saw two problems at once with this arrangement: d_ ArkAngl would be living with an exotic woman of wealth and beauty, and the woman he'd be living with was dangerous. She addressed the danger issue first.

"Isn't that playing with fire? GlobeCom's watching you all the time, and you let one of them into your home—your bedroom even?" she asked, concerned.

"Keep your enemies close," he replied sardonically.

"So, then, are you already sleeping with this Ying?" she asked testily. "Is she beautiful and petite and exotic with glossy black hair? Do you think of her every night like you say you think of me?"

"Jealousy is beneath you, my darling," he responded gently. "You know I will love you always, deeply, and no one will ever come close to you in my heart."

"So … she'd be the one who everyone sees you with in public. I am the hidden one," Cy added sadly. "She is the one who will be with you every day, doing normal things, while I get just these stolen moments."

"Ah, but they're damn good stolen moments," he said, kissing her lightly on the neck and nibbling her ear. "And yes, she will go to the ball games with me and make me dinner," he continued, putting his arms around her and holding her close to his heart. "But *you*. You are my soul wife. Don't ever forget that. Not to mention, you are the mother of what will be my only child."

Cy pulled away for a second, looked him in the eyes again, questioning. "Wait. How do you know this will be your only child?"

"Because I already took care of that, medically speaking. I refuse to bring another human into a world where personal freedom is impossible," he said.

Cy started crying softly.

"This separation is going to be so hard. My … My head gets it … but my heart doesn't," she said between sniffles.

"I also see you growing closer to Des," he observed, trying not to let his own jealousy rise up.

"He's been a gentleman all the way," Cy defended. "But you are right. We're making it appear already as if we are a couple and that he is father to Adam. Sickening to me."

"It sickens me too," he answered, choking up a little. "I mean, Des, not I, helped you deliver *our* baby. That is a level of intimacy that goes beyond acting. And I will always envy him for that experience. Even though we devised this plan and set it up this way, it still cuts me to the core."

"Then we both feel bad," said Cy.

"We both feel bad," he echoed.

Eighteen months later, Michael came to her, and for a short time, Cy was mother of two boys under the age of two.

It was a hot day in June, so Cy took the babies outside early in the morning to work on the garden. She was nursing six-month-old Michael on a stump just outside the garden gate when Adam, nearly two, toddled into the fenced-in garden and reached for a green tomato on the vine. Cy tried to stop him, but she was too late.

"No, no, little Adam. Don't pick that yet. It's not ripe," she said. "It needs to be red ..."

Adam, with a full head of curly strawberry blond hair, took a bite of the green tomato. Then, finding it too sour for his taste, he spit it out, the green juice dribbling down the front of his white shirt. He decided to bring the rest of the tomato to Cy, presenting it to her as if it was a precious gift.

"Why thank you, little Adam," Cy said, accepting the gift like she was royalty.

Just then, Adam looked up to the sky directly above them, a curious expression crossing his face. Baby Michael also pulled from her breast and twisted his head to look the same direction as Adam's gaze. As Cy's eyes slowly followed theirs, she dropped the tomato and gasped.

Just a mere fifteen feet above them, she saw a flickering of light as if a mirror was in the sky, and it dawned on her that she was looking at a new type of drone, silent and camouflaged. It hovered directly above them, blinking in and out of visibility, changing with the color of the sky and the trees around it.

This was *not* one of Des's drones.

"Ho-ly shit," she exclaimed, protectively pulling Adam to her knee.

Just then, Des's voice crackled over her wrist comm. "We see the drone. Whatever you do, do *not* look up."

"Too late. We are already totally owned," Cy said into her

comm. "Whoever's controlling that thing has seen and recorded all of our attributes."

She examined the drone.

"Interesting. It has adaptive camouflage. Nearly impossible to see," she observed. "And silent. Not just quiet. But silent. You cannot hear any rotors running. I wonder how it stays in the sky."

Inside the computer workroom, Des and Bilbo's sensors were going crazy.

"How did it get through our defenses? We should have detected it at the property edge, even if we couldn't physically see or hear it," Bilbo said, somewhat disgusted with their own tech.

"This is a new type of drone pinging a unique signal. Our scramblers appear to be useless at detecting unknown drone signals or channels. This *will not* do," Des answered as he rushed to the supply room. "You stay here and power everything down. I'm stopping this sucker the old-fashioned way."

Awareness dawned across Bilbo's bearded face.

"Shit. Oh, shit. OK. OK," Bilbo said hastily. "I'm shutting systems down now. But please close the panic door on your way out to keep the pulse from leaking in here and killing our electronics."

"Roger that," Des responded as he grabbed the EMP gun from the rack.

Out in the glen, Cy and the babies were still looking up, their eyes trying to track the drone. Des's voice sounded over her wrist comm again.

"We're downloading data on the device now. What's it doing?" he asked.

The drone shivered and quaked above her, as if it were readying itself for something.

"I don't know, but now might be a good time for us to get the hell out of here," she said.

Keeping Michael cradled in her left arm, she swooped Adam up onto her right hip, and with the superhuman strength of a mother protecting her children, she sprinted the length of the small clearing, feeling as if her feet weren't even touching the ground.

"I'm leading it away from our cave. Heading for the bomb shelter in the woods," she said breathlessly over her wrist comm.

Des appeared out in front of the cave and aimed the EMP gun directly at the drone. But before he could fire, a loud voice with an Irish accent shouted at them through the drone's speakers.

"Don't shoot this drone. Don't shoot the drone! It's a gift. Courtesy of CL0 clan."

Des, immediately relieved, powered down his EMP as the drone uncamouflaged itself and safely landed on the stump Cy had previously occupied. Cy stopped at the edge of the forest and turned back to see they were no longer in danger. Michael and Adam were crying in her arms.

"It's OK, babies. It's OK. We're safe. We're all safe," she said, her heart beating wildly in her chest as she tried to calm them and herself down.

Adam sniffled and then looked toward the parking garage just as Skew emerged with a drone controller in hand.

"Unna skoo, unna skoo," Adam said, squirming to get back down on the ground.

Skew, at thirty-three, was the practical joker and full-on Irish with all the attributes. This day, he was wearing jeans and sneakers, unlike the first time Cy met him when he was in a kilt.

Cy let the wiggling Adam down, and he dashed back toward the garden to intercept Skew and Des.

"How did you? How did ..." Des started to ask Skew.

"How'd I get past your security? I knew your passcodes to your local network, so flying in plain sight was easy enough," Skew offered. "Although, I *did* have to hack your video cams to hide my own self coming here through the woods. You guys need to work on that."

Adam hugged Skew's leg affectionately, and Cy caught up with them, still breathing heavy. She was pissed. With her one free hand, she started punching Skew on the shoulder like she would hit an annoying brother.

"You scared the hell out of me! And our kids!" she scolded.

"Unna. Unna," said Adam, reaching up to Skew. "Want unna."

Skew picked Adam up for hug and nuzzled him with his long red beard, much to Adam's delight.

"The little lads don't seem too upset," Skew said. "In fact, master Adam here looks very happy to see his Uncle Skew."

"I almost fried that thing. I could have ruined the drone," Des objected.

"Yeah, but you didn't because I was watching," Skew responded.

Adam started squirming again, so Skew set him down while Cy handed Michael over to Des and tried to catch her breath.

"Man, you should have seen Cy's face when she thought she was owned," Skew said, laughing till he almost cried. "Seriously funny."

"Again. Not ... funny ... Skew," Cy said, trying not to hit him some more.

"C'mon! It was so so, so, soooo funny," Skew said, sidling up to Cy. "You know you love me. Now give us a hug."

Skew lifted Cy up off her feet in a bearhug and gave her back a nice little chiropractic crack before putting her down again.

"Now, don't you feel better? You always love when I do that," he offered.

Cy just glared at him.

"Still nothing? Well, here's my excuse: It was easier just to fly this thing here rather than carry it. Honestly, I didn't realize you'd be outside with the little lads here. The opportunity just, um, presented itself when I saw you there," he explained.

Des was examining the drone, bird-shaped and about three feet at its largest wingspan and built more like an airplane with small turbines in the wings. He also noted ports and adapters for weapons and cameras.

"Looks extremely aerodynamic," Des said. "We've got us some reverse engineering to do."

Cy gave Des a sour look. "Ah, yes. Take *his* side now." Then to Skew, she added. "How did you even get this?"

"Ah, tools of the trade, my dear. Don't ask, don't tell," Skew answered. "But I can say this is GlobeCom's latest armed observation drone, *still beta*—not out in general use yet. We've even got the user's guide, specs, and manufacturing guide right here, in print."

Skew removed his backpack and pulled out two softback user manuals. "They're using proprietary signal channels and never-before-seen cloaking tech," he continued. "We need to learn how to train our systems to see these things when they come around, so I thought the best man to do that would be your Des. Hell, if Des is as good as everyone says, he can remote control any one of GlobeCom's drones using their own tech against them."

"Um ... Thank you? I think?" Des responded.

Adam started tugging on Cy's leg impatiently.

"Humidity's rising," she said to all of them. "We should go inside for some refreshments, although I'm tempted to leave Uncle Skew out here in the heat."

"I'm crushed," said Skew, hand to heart, feigning heartbreak. "But seriously, what are you cooking in there today?"

"Cy and I would love for you to join us for refreshments," Des offered, ignoring Cy's disapproving look.

Skew accepted the offer readily. "Oh, good. I thought you'd never ask. I'm parched."

Skew put on his backpack and collected the drone, grunting as he lifted it.

"How long can you stay?" Des asked him.

"I can only stay a day or two. I have a new lass back home about to birth a babe," Skew replied. "Lost my first wife, Elven's mother, as you know, during childbirth. So, I plan to be there for this one."

"Wow. You move fast," Cy responded, impressed. "Even living off-grid, you find no shortage of willing females."

"What can I say? I cannot run a home without a good woman," he said, smiling back at her. "My lady says she feels like she's carrying a girl, so we want to name her Saoirse. Pronounced *Seersha*."

"That's a beautiful name. What does it mean?" asked Des.

"It means freedom," Skew answered.

CHAPTER 8.

PUPPET MASTERS

PRESENT DAY

Leonard and Ying are preparing breakfast at the kitchen bar in their modern Beijing high-rise. Stock market data from the global exchanges scrolls endlessly in a floating plasma display between them. The statistics and trade data are latent representations of what was actually happening in the market twelve hours ago—the best she could get with GlobeCom down. The numbers are drastically downward, sending off a colorful array of alarms that Ying and Leonard seem numb to.

Ying is preparing a simple breakfast of egg yolks on rice. The rising sun filters through floor-to-ceiling windows beside her and highlights the subtle blue tint in her glossy black hair. It also shines through her thin silk robe, revealing a slight, trim body that gives her the look of a twenty-year-old rather than the forty-two-year-old she is.

Leonard admires her graceful movement as she drops some chopped green onions on top of the warm, runny yolks.

"You were wonderful last night," he says. "And a hot breakfast this morning? To what do I owe the many honors?"

"Things are so chaotic right now, and I just felt we both need some TLC," she says with an accent that sounds more British than Chinese.

She sets the bowls down on their bamboo placemats and looks nervously at the stock market numbers jumping around on the screen.

"It's been ten days now, and I'm still reverting to this archaic method of trying to track the crashing markets," she says, frustrated.

Her normally calming and authoritative voice sounds shaky and worried, and she has reason to worry—for the both of them. She's no idiot, which is why Leonard fell in love with her. Her British accent is a leftover from her formative years in boarding school at Cheltenham, Gloucestershire, followed by five more years taking dual majors in law and economics at Oxford. She still holds her license to practice financial law in England, while also passing the bar and maintaining her legal status in the United States and in China. She's the perfect mix of brains and beauty that Leonard is drawn to.

Leonard scoops some of the rice mixture into his mouth and savors it.

"Delicious as always, my darling," he says after tasting it.

"Thank you, my dear," she responds fondly. "I'm also feeding us so well because I'm being called to New York today."

"Why?" he asks, surprised at the suddenness of her trip.

"To check on the markets and meet with the Federal Reserve board," she answers.

"Oh, of course. I should have realized that," he responds. "So, you'll be taking the ultrasonic?"

"Yes. It's still flying, if that's what you're asking. The pilots are trained to use manual navigations in case they ever fall out of autopilot. And they're using old-fashioned radio channels to talk with towers who reverted to radar for landing and takeoff," she explains. "So far, no one's crashing any planes, although there are far fewer in the sky."

"I wish you didn't have to go," Leonard says, meaning it. "I just don't feel right about you taking this trip, especially when I've got the entire GlobeCom board breathing down my neck as if *I* caused this somehow—even if not directly, maybe inadvertently through sloppy protocols."

"This is not just about you," she says, a little testily. "The board is bearing down on the both of us. I've not been requested so much as demanded to take this trip."

He looks at her pensively, not sure how to tell her he's scared as shit, but she seems to get the message.

"Don't worry. We have our honored mother, Nǚ Jiāzhǎng," she reminds him. "Under her protection, we should be OK."

Ying's strength in the midst of their vulnerability is intoxicating to Leonard, who sets down his chopsticks and brushes his hand against her pale shoulder.

"After all these years, you are still the total package, and I cannot get enough of you quivering in my arms," he says as he drops her robe off her shoulder, revealing her small but firm breasts.

Ying twists her stool to face him, smiling lustily.

"If you think that's going to get me in the mood again, you're right," she says, leaning forward and grasping his face between her hands and then kissing it all over.

She leans back and spreads her legs as she opens the rest of her robe. "Now, show me one more time how much you love me."

The next day, Leonard looks a mess in his boxers and five o'clock shadow as he stares at the empty plasma screen. He's trying to reach Ying, who's not accepting his connection requests. He's also been trying to reach her sisters and honored mother. He should be able to connect to all of them through the local towers—but only if they are on his continent.

He heads to the bedroom where his suitcase is open on their platform bed and continues packing.

"Where are you Ying? You're not responding," he says to himself. "And now, I've been ordered to DC."

TWELVE YEARS EARLIER

From his opulent, mahogany-paneled office in London, Damian Strand watched everything and everyone who piqued his interest. As head of the GlobeCom board, he had access to all the digital assets his heart desired. And for the most part, what he wanted was information that would give him *more* power and control.

Damian wasn't much of a looker. His mousy brown hair was already thinning, and he was average height and build. But there was a dark intensity in his eyes that drew people to him.

On his private screen, Damian had an open syndicate file from the Circle, a secret organization that he'd set up to run all things on the darknet. To the public, GlobeCom was cleaning up this filthy underbelly of the network, referred to as the darknet and sometimes called the undernet. But behind the curtain, Strand, under the anonymous handle of DarkL0rd, simply organized criminals into syndicates with a blood-backed pledge of absolute allegiance to the DarkL0rd.

To join the Circle, every member of every crime ring swore a blood oath not to divulge its existence. Criminals and crime groups who chose not to join the Circle simply disappeared, while the glory went to GlobeCom for ridding the darknet of the crime ring scum. Only organized syndicates were allowed into the Circle, and if anyone from the syndicates divulged the existence or any information about the Circle under *any* circumstance, their entire syndicate, and those in each member's personal, familial, and business circles would disappear, their assets reallocated to wherever the DarkL0rd saw fit to use them.

This day, Damian had the Little Angels syndicate file open on his screen. He needed a fall group, and the Little Angels syndicate was going under that bus for two reasons. First, their crimes were heinous enough to stir the masses and the GlobeCom leadership into accepting that which they normally couldn't. And second, Damian never felt OK with the pedo rings. They really did disgust him, despite the hefty cut that they brought into the Circle. Better to run with clean crimes like drugs, money laundering, counterfeit, gambling, and prostitution.

"Get this pedophile scum out of the syndicates while achieving the higher goal," Damian said to himself with a hard-to-place mixed European accent. "I'd call that a win-win."

He closed the syndicate's files, which erased their traces and burrowed back into their secret and masked locations distributed across a secured, hidden cloud. Then he opened his private window into Adrianna's inner sanctum where he had pin cameras hidden everywhere without her knowledge. He scrolled through the feeds from Adrianna's bedroom, dressing area, living room, and kitchen, eventually finding her in her office. Then he switched to his official GlobeCom channel and video called her.

"Connect to Adrianna Dupres," Damian said to his wall device.

In a few seconds, Adrianna, looking as put together and poised as ever, appeared on the screen.

"Misère Damian. To what do I owe the honor?" she asked, smiling warmly.

"Greetings, mademoiselle. I hope that you and the babe are well," he answered formally.

"Yes, thank you. We are fine here," Adrianna responded. "But my Stonces is no babe anymore. He is seven years old, excelling at all of his courses, and he's a natural with computers like his father."

"That is nice to hear, nice to hear," Damian said, seeming distracted. "Listen. I bring bad news, I'm afraid. It's sickening news, actually."

Her body shifted uncomfortably as she braced for the news.

"Investigators found another criminal group on the darknet," he explained as gently as he could. "This one wasn't selling knockoff watches or illegal gambling. It was much, much worse. It served pedophiles on the black market for very little boys even younger than your son's age."

Adrianna felt a punch in her gut and thought she was going to puke. Instead, she started cussing in French for a full two minutes, as if she had Tourette's, shouting so loud that Damian had to turn his volume down.

Finally, she collected herself enough to speak. "What are we doing about it?" she asked shakily.

"It gets worse," he said. "Some of these little boys didn't survive their ordeals."

"Heinous! Deranged, debauched! Those poor children!" she screamed before crying loudly.

She reached for a tissue on her desk, dropping out of view of the screen for a moment to blow her nose and dab her eyes. She came back to face him again.

"Have we apprehended these depraved animals?" she asked. "Can we get the operators and the, the ... How do you call them in English? ... The johns?"

"Yes. And we turned evidence over to law enforcement. I just wanted you to know it will be big news when it breaks, most likely tomorrow or the day after," he answered somberly. "There were several pimps, all of them rounded up, and the johns are still being collected."

"It is sickening, you are right," she said, dabbing her eyes again. "These cybercriminal enterprises, they keep popping up like … How do you say? … Like Whac-A-Mole."

"That is true. But the more we make an example of them, the better the deterrent," Damian coaxed, gently pushing Adrianna toward a decision he wanted her to make on her own.

"So, you are thinking capital punishment this time?" she asked. "This would be our first cybercase to test the global death penalty."

"Based on the evidence I was briefed on, yes," he responded. "There will likely be more than one in the group from more than one country to face capital charges."

"Understood," she acknowledged. "We need a meeting of the board. And we need to get all our social media partners ready. Let me make some calls."

"Thank You, Adrianna," he answered.

Instead of disconnecting as he should have, Damian paused awkwardly, and Adrianna looked at him quizzically.

"And, um, one more thing, if you please," he said finally. "I'd like the honor of getting to know you better. May I look you up for dinner the next time we're in the same location?"

When she didn't answer immediately, he stumbled around. "I mean, I don't want to presume you're over the loss of your husband, but it's been almost five years, but I also know that everyone takes their own time."

His discomfort amused her and briefly took her mind away from the horrors they'd just discussed.

"Oh, sir. You must be the last great gentleman," she said,

smiling lightly through her tears. "I will accept such an offer—if, as you say, we're ever in the same city long enough."

After their communication disconnected, Damian switched views to the DC hub, where security manager Ron Meeker was coordinating a video meeting between GlobeCom's three lead CSOs hailing from the DC, China, and Euro-Arab hubs.

From his screen, Damian heard and saw everything, including details emanating from the meeting attendees' UIs.

Damian checked into this call between the CSOs a little early to find Ron Meeker, from the DC hub, and Leonard Smith, the Beijing CSO, having a friendly catch-up conversation before the Euro-Arab CSO logged in.

"Can't wait to be there on your big day, and thanks for the accommodations," Meeker said enthusiastically. "Happy to be your best man, and my wife and kids can't wait to see you again in person."

"Two weeks, and we tie the knot," Leonard responded. "Seems so far away and yet so close ..."

"You worried?" Meeker asked, kiddingly.

"Me? Worried? About what? Marrying into the most influential family in Beijing?" Leonard answered playfully. "All the sisters, aunts, uncles, cousins, nieces, and nephews? Um, noooo problem."

"Yeah, I figured that was why you were engaged for so long." Meeker laughed.

Damian checked Leonard's vitals. Something about that man was just too put together, and he didn't trust the guy. Yet, he saw that Leonard's vitals were all in order for the discussion they were having about the beautiful and intelligent Ying Liu, including the slight rise in Leonard's blood pressure.

"No, really, I am happy," Leonard continued, meaning it. "Living alone in a big and foreign city kind of sucks, actually. And I couldn't do better for a brilliant life partner and loving spouse ... But enough about me! How's your growing family?"

CHAPTER 9.

HOUSE OF YING

PRESENT DAY

Adrianna Dupres, fifty-three, sits elegantly on an overstuffed sofa in the posh living room of her classic country chateau. Across from her, Ying is perched on a fourteenth-century armchair while sipping from a steaming cup of tea.

"Thank you, my dear, for coming. Your husband, he does not know you are here, no?" Adrianna asks.

"He thinks I'm in New York at a meeting with the Reserve," Ying answers.

"Good, good," Adrianna responds, a little distracted.

Rather than her normal cordial self, Adrianna seems intense today. Of course, who isn't? With all of GlobeCom down, their entire operation is in turmoil, and the whole world is in chaos.

Adrianna takes a sip of her scotch and then sets the crystal highball back down on her onyx coffee table. "There *must* be an inside person," insists Adrianna, her French accent a little more pronounced than normal. "How else would they know *where* to strike? And with such *precision?*"

"Whoever it was, I don't know," Ying says honestly. "But it seems that they took advantage of weaknesses even we didn't know we had."

"And that's another thing. We pay our security people a lot of money to keep our systems protected, no? So why were we not protected?" Adrianna continues, her voice slightly raising. "How does our security fail on such a global, catastrophic scale?"

Ying suddenly realizes where this is going and why she was brought here. She gets a sinking feeling in her stomach but says nothing, not wanting to stoke the fires growing in Adrianna's eyes.

As if reading her thoughts, Adrianna continues, "One of the IT leaders is your husband, no? Leonard Smith—he is one of our CSOs, works in the China hub. Tell me about him."

Feeling protective, Ying responds cautiously. "I'm sure Leonard had nothing to do with this," Ying answers. "Right now, he's working like a mad man to find out who's responsible and make repairs. We are both losing sleep over all of this."

"Yes, yes, I understand," Adrianna responds, not really caring. "Tell me … has he … Has Leonard Smith been acting suspicious lately?"

Ying senses a calculated coldness she's never seen in Adrianna before. Gone is the graceful auntie who Ying used to know, and in her place is a master interrogator.

"Nothing really stands out," Ying answers, trying to stay calm. "He's been a little more loving these past few days, but he says I've been spoiling him more than normal too. So, I don't know what to tell you …"

"We've just ordered him to a meeting of the CSOs in DC so he can sort this out for us," Adrianna shares.

"I see," says Ying thoughtfully. "All of the CSOs are going? Including the CSO from the Euro-Arab Hub? Will she also be there?"

"She's currently stuck in the Moscow office coordinating the investigation with Director Strand," Adrianna responds.

"So, you're rounding up all the CSOs but the Euro-Arab CSO? That doesn't make sense. If I were to pick any insider behind this, it would be someone from Russia," Ying advises.

For a split second, Adrianna looks culpable and then defensive while still maintaining her smooth sense of elegance.

"That's none of your affair, my beauty," Adrianna answers. "I'm just asking about the man you know—your husband. Maybe we can avoid any unnecessary unpleasantries in DC if we uncover the traitor here and now."

Ying fights off a sense of dread and panic, worried as much for herself as for her husband.

"Is this why you brought me here under false pretenses? Thinking I had dirt on my husband?" Ying answers, growing angry. "Well I don't. You need to stand down from this plan. These IT directors ... They have families. They are loyal and work long hours in a thankless job where if something goes wrong, it's always their fault. Hell, I'm married to one and am but his mistress, where GlobeCom is his master. You need these CSOs now more than ever."

"Ridding our IT ranks of some of the more useless or culpable people would set an example. It would also motivate those left behind to find our attackers in record time," Adrianna argues.

"Nǚ Jiāzhǎng, honored mother, will not allow the rounding up any of our region's IT experts, particularly my husband, who is like a son to her," Ying challenges.

At that moment, Adrianna's nineteen-year-old son, Stonces, enters the room. Clean-cut, dark-skinned, tall, and strong with model-good looks, Stonces has an air of confidence beyond his age.

Ying stands to greet him, her arms extended. "Stonces! You're all grown up. Give us a hug!" she says.

"Auntie Ying! Nice to see you again. I didn't know you were here," he responds, happy to see her.

He bends down to scoop her into his arms, and they embrace affectionately. She then steps back to check him out like an auntie would.

"A strapping young man! You look amazing," Ying says. "How's Yale? How long has it been?"

"I think it's been five years since I've seen you, Auntie," he answers in perfect English with a light French accent. "I'm nineteen now, been I've been in university for almost four years."

"Started early, I see," Ying says, proud of him. "Not surprising given how bright you are. So, what brings you home midsemester?"

"Schools are closed for the moment on account of GlobeCom being down. I'm here for now, helping out my lovely mother," he says, taking a seat on the couch next to Adrianna.

"Hello, darling," Adrianna says, giving Stonces a peck on the cheek. "It is good to have you here with me during these hard times."

"So, I couldn't help overhearing at the door about your dilemma," Stonces observes. "Mind if I interject an idea?"

Adrianna nods affirmatively.

"I think you need your own insider to infiltrate the clans, and that insider should be me. I have the skills and the youth to pass for one of them," he suggests.

"Wonderful idea, my dear!" Adrianna beams. "I will bring that to the board. Although right now, it is harder to reach them with comm channels down."

"And your communications systems should be one of the first tasks that your IT pros are motivated to fix," Ying offers.

"Stonces, love, what's the latest report on that?" Adrianna asks.

"Oh God, it's still a mess out there," Stonces answers. "Half the communication satellites are destroyed, and the other half are damaged and, for now, useless. Others, like our weather and navigation satellites, were left intact. We might be able to repurpose them, but that will be slow. For now, we're going back to old-school IP transport through local cell towers. So, you know, obsolete technology will have to hold us over."

"Won't you need a lot of reprogramming to do that? And do we even have anyone who uses those old programming languages, like Java?" Adrianna asks.

"Your knowledge of old tech is impressive, Mom!" Stonces acknowledges approvingly. "The skills are hard to find, but we have some in the work camps."

Just then, two men from Adrianna's security detail walk in.

"Speaking of work camps," Adrianna says so cold it sends a chill through Ying's spine. "So, Ying, darling … Loved catching up with you, but now it's time for you to go."

Without warning, the guards pull Ying from her chair, causing her to drop the expensive gilded teacup, which shatters noisily on the Italian tile floor.

"What? Don't touch me! What are you doing? What the hell *is* this?" Ying shouts as she wiggles to get her arms loose from the guards.

"Nothing personal," Adrianna says without emotion. "But I can think of no better motivation for your husband to tell the truth than having you locked up in a work camp, no? Particularly if he learns you are in Camp 74."

Ying's face goes pale. She suddenly feels dizzy and nauseated.

"No! Not *that* hell hole! You have no right or authority to do this," Ying objects. Ying throws a pleading look at Stonces and then feels crushed as he looks on impassively.

"Sorry, Auntie. You're a peach," he responds. "But I never did like that husband of yours. He's shifty. And far too full of himself, if you ask me."

"Nǚ Jiāzhǎng, honored mother, will never stand for this!" Ying shouts.

"Your honored mother and your entire family are already taken care of in separate camps throughout the Euro-Arab territories," Adrianna answers.

"Impossible. Honored mother is protected by an army of ten thousand guards and soldiers!" Ying spits.

"Yes, sorry about your soldiers and guards," Adrianna says sardonically. "Those we couldn't turn have been eliminated or detained. More of them detained than eliminated, if that helps. Nobody wants to recklessly take human lives."

"No, you just control them instead," Ying hisses, feeling heavy and groggy.

Ying twists and kicks clumsily as if through quicksand, while Adrianna's goons drag her from the room. As they pull her through the double doors into the foyer, Ying uses her final bit of strength to tap on her familial spirits.

"You will be sorry for this," Ying slurs. "I join my honored mother and relatives, living and dead. A family curse to you and all you love!"

"I won't hold that against you, darling," Adrianna replies, a plastic smile on her face. "Enjoy your sleep."

Ying goes limp as the doors close behind her. Then Stonces turns to his mother.

"So, why are we taking over the China hub?" he asks.

"Well, darling, if you must know, we're absorbing her family's vast holdings to create GlobeCom 2.0 and finish our new AI. Also, we need their programming capacity," she responds, swishing the last of her scotch and finishing it. "Besides, I think we're better off with fewer board stakes to compete with. And that, dear son, is where you come in."

"So … Get rid of the competition? Locate the other board members' assets, transfer them to us, find their weaknesses? I'm in!" he answers a little too eagerly. "I'm assuming you want me to leave uncle Damian alone, though, right?"

She leans forward and sets the glass down.

"Yes, don't touch Damian," she instructs.

"Damian's been good to us, so I wouldn't go after him even if you asked me to," he adds. "No offense, Mother."

"None taken," she says, smiling for the first time in days.

"Before you start that task, please take extra steps to protect our assets and our lives," she continues. "The board is starting to unravel. I've already converted most of our digital monies into gold and platinum, and I've hired extra physical security presence. I suggest you don't go anywhere without a guard."

"First thing I'll do is change all of our passcodes and upgrade our rotating firewalls and sniffers," he offers.

"Yes, that sounds like an important place to start," she agrees. "Also, please locate and protect the AI development for GlobeCom 2.0. We need the full AI, not just parts of it."

"But the AI development is spread all over the place, particularly on the work camp servers," he responds. "It'll be hard to collect all of that."

"Start with Camp 74," she says. "The largest development group is working there under some savant amnesiac who looks like a hobbit."

TEN YEARS EARLIER

An unshaven and barefoot Bilbo, thirty-seven, looked disoriented and scared. He was strapped down to a simulator chair and hooked up to the EMBIR (pronounced "ember"), which stands for electromagnetic brain image reader. He didn't seem to know where—or who—he was.

The small room with dingy cinder block walls smelled of must and tobacco. Two men dressed in army-green coveralls sat at a worn-looking metal desk in the corner by the door, trying to figure him out.

The older, darker man was looking into a computer screen, scrutinizing the brain images projected from the EMBIR. He spoke limited English and perfect Russian.

"We are only seeing little, just a small little brain activity in zee EMBIR. Except for fear regions … I see big activity there," said the Russian. "Is my EMBIR broken? Diagnostics say EMBIR is working."

"Well, it's Chinese tech, so you never know," answered the other man, an American who spoke perfect English with limited Russian.

"Can … Can I have some water please? My mouth is so dry," Bilbo finally managed to ask.

"We have you on IV for fluid. You should be hydrating nicely about now," said the American who was about thirty years old with a slight frame, blond hair, and blue eyes.

The American turned his attention back to the screen, looking over the Russian's shoulder at the map of Bilbo's brain. "I mean, this can't be right," he argued. "The only thing visibly lighting up are his fear and pain centers. Where the hell is the rest of his mind?"

The Russian guard turned from the screen and looked at Bilbo, who'd been intently staring at their computer interface and trying to figure out what was going on.

"Call medical doctor," the Russian said into his wrist comm.

The computer answered in a Dolly Parton voice. "Yes, sir, will getchya a medical doctor pronto. Which doctor wouldya like me to connect you with, pardner?"

The American, impatient, piped in, "Just get us whoever's available at this moment."

"Hold on there, cowboy! You are not authorized to direct me," the computer responded, making the American even more impatient.

"Please send nearest available doctor," the Russian ordered, gloating at his American counterpart. "Attach request with this case file on-screen."

"Sure thing, pardner. File has been sent," the computer said in its most cheerful Dolly Parton voice. "Doctor confirmed. ETA in sixty-seven seconds."

Finally, Bilbo recognized something—the voice. It belonged to someone important to him. Who could she be? As he remembered, the happiness center of Bilbo's brain lit up in the interface.

"I ... I know that computer voice," Bilbo said, trying to think. "She's ... She's famous, right? I can almost see her ..."

"He seems know who zee Dolly Parton was, ya? Greatest woman ever lived," the Russian said as the American nodded in agreement.

"Look at his brain light up," said the American. "He must have a thing for her like you do!"

The door opened, and a female doctor in her forties entered the small room. She wore a white lab coat over a sweater and jeans and had auburn hair that fell to her shoulders.

The doctor looked at Bilbo and then raised an eyebrow at the Russian, who stood and offered her his chair. He seemed to have a little crush on her.

The doctor politely ignored the offer of the chair, instead stepping toward Bilbo and asking in perfect English, "Why was I called in? And why does he have no shoes on?"

"Um, he arrived that way," said the American.

This new inmate had huge feet—and so hairy. She'd never seen so much hair on feet before. She touched the leathery soles and then his toes. They were *warm*—a gift she wished she possessed as she looked down at her fleece-lined boots.

"Here's new one for you, Doctor," said the Russian. "Diz hobbit man here, he put parts of his brain in zee sleep mode. We cannot see any other activity on zee EMBIR but for zee fear center."

The American confirmed, adding, "He's right, Doc. There's no hack for erasing the brain, is there? I mean, he has no chip, no implants of any kind anywhere—like he never had one. So we called you."

"Did you run his DNA sequence?" asked the doctor, who sounded like she was from the Midwest, likely somewhere in Iowa.

"We are processing that now, but matching records don't seem to exist," the American answered. "He may have gone off-grid before we fully populated the national DNA databases. I don't know."

"That would have been a long while ago," she answered, thinking.

"So long ago that he'd have much intel for us, no?" said the Russian opportunistically. "We need to get zee intel out of his brain."

The doctor checked Bilbo's pulse. "His pulses are all over the place. He's shit-scared. You're right about his fear centers," she said. "We don't need the EMBIR to show us that."

Leaning down to Bilbo, she tried to calm him. "Sir, you say you have no recollection of who you are and how you came to be here?" she asked, using her best friendly voice.

Bilbo looked up at her, lost and pleading with his eyes. "Yes, ma'am. That's what I've been trying to tell these two here, um, whatever they are."

"They are rehabilitation experts from GlobeCom," she answered gently. "We're at Camp 74, and these are your counselors."

Bilbo stared at her blankly, still not understanding or recognizing anything she was saying.

"You do know what GlobeCom is, don't you?" she asked.

"Not sure I do, ma'am," Bilbo answered, trying to think and

then getting a severe headache. "Seems … Seems, um, vaguely familiar. But when I try to remember, all I see is fuzz."

"Fuzz? Explain what you mean by fuzz," the doctor asked.

"It's like those old TVs from the 1970s, the ones with the antenna ears that would blink black, white, and gray fuzz when you click to a channel where there's no station. That kind of fuzz. Trying to remember makes the fuzz worse, and it makes my head hurt."

"He's not lying about the pain part," the American said, reading from pain centers lighting up on the EMBIR image.

The doctor looked amused. She took a penlight from her chest pocket and pointed it into Bilbo's eyes. His pupils reacted too slowly. Then she turned off the light, dimmed the room, and his pupils stayed as small as pinpricks. She turned the lights back on and aligned her finger in front of his eyes.

"Do you see my finger? Follow my finger," she instructed.

Bilbo's eyes didn't track well, jerking side to side rapidly like he was having some type of spasm. She made note of it on her wrist comm and then turned to the interrogators.

"Tell me, how long has he been here?" she asked.

"Twenty hours in travel plus four hours here recovering. He was out the entire time until about an hour ago," said the American.

"Travel? I traveled? *From* where? And *to* where?" Bilbo asked, desperately.

"Well, his intellect and vocabulary seem intact," said the doctor, pulling a blood capture kit from her bag. "Now, I need to take a blood test and run some additional scans. If my hunch is right, his memories may be unrecoverable."

CHAPTER 10.

STEPPING UP

PRESENT DAY

Allure is beside herself with worry as she paces back and forth in the small living space she shares with Mane. Her unitard is especially tight today and is a glossy bloodred color to match her stilettos. Bloodred (with golden-yellow accents) is also the dominant color in rugs and silks she draped around the shack to conceal computer components and old barn walls she finds so discordant with her visual flair.

Allure is fuming (anger being her normal reaction to fear). Mane must have run off to the Watergate on this half-baked plan without so much as telling her. He went with Skew of *all people*.

"Reckless!" she says to herself. "No note, no explanation, no see you later, honey."

She stops pacing and tries his comm again. Nothing—which

means he's most definitely off-property. And she knows instinctively he's gone to the Watergate.

"You're going to get yourself killed, you idiot," she says to the empty room.

Across the property, Wizard shakes Cy awake at noon. It's the day after the memorial service for Des.

"Mistress, mistress!" Wizard says urgently as he wakes her. "I think Mane and Skew took a crew to go after Leonard in DC while we were all sleeping."

"What? What?" Cy asks.

She attempts to sit up before remembering she can't sit without help. So Cy shifts herself to her side, facing the edge of the bed, and then pushes up with her arms into a partial sitting position while Wizard sets her feet on the floor.

"Did d_ArkAngl get our warning message?" she asks.

"I don't know. He should get it if he's landing anywhere near the DC area," Wizard explains as he helps position Cy for transfer to her chair. "Are you ready?"

After the transfer, Cy completes her first feat of the day, the morning routine which takes three times longer than when she had the use of her legs. Then she wheels into the workroom where her computers turn on and idle, waiting for her commands. She's wearing one of Des's T-shirts with pull-on sweatpants, the best she could do given that her lower body is dead weight.

Her mind swims with fear and regret. How does she tell any of her fellow clan people that Leonard Smith is their mole when he's still inside GlobeCom and being closely watched? She's deep in thought as Wizard rolls up in a work chair beside her.

"Our boy's still under the thumb of GlobeCom, so you

couldn't tell anybody at the group last night who he really is," Wizard says, as if reading her mind.

"Well, maybe I should have pulled Skew aside instead of going with you to warn him," Cy says. "Maybe we should have—"

"This is hindsight, and it is not productive, mistress …" Wizard interjects. "We need a constructive plan, and we need it now."

"I'm at a loss as to how to prevent yet another catastrophe," Cy says. "My mind is like sludge, and my heart … It's a deep hole, and I think it's impacting my mind."

"I feel the same, mistress. Des was one of a kind," Wizard responds. "You need to eat. That should help."

He places a plate with a walnut-apple turnover stuffed with sweetened goat cheese on the table beside her. "Michael made a large tray of these for this morning's breakfast, thinking there'd be at least a dozen people left over from last night's service," Wizard offers.

"The boys! Where are they?" Cy asks, suddenly realizing they aren't in their room. "They didn't go with Mane and Skew, did they?"

"Madame, they are all safe and accounted for," Wizard reports, calming her. "Found the younglings in a pile of sleeping bags at the old bomb shelter on the way over here. R3x is with them, along with an empty bottle of moonshine. So they'll be out for a while. I can't find Elven, though, so he must have gone with the adults."

"Adults," Cy says with an ironic chuckle. "Skew and Mane are the *least* adult among us."

"Eat, mistress. Eat," Wizard advises.

A few bites of the warm, delicious turnover revive her a bit. Now, she needs some coffee to clear the fog.

As if reading her mind again, Wizard hands Cy a cup of dark coffee the way she likes—no cream, no sugar. She sets her plate on the worktable next to her, picks up the mug, and holds it in both hands, savoring the smell before taking a sip.

"Leonard is heading right into their trap at the Washington hub," she says, finally able to think again. "And I anticipate some real bad actors are already in play, like, say Damian Strand and his goons? Does anyone on the board even know he's a Russian operative pulling all their strings?"

"Well, we do," Wizard replies. "Just no safe way to leak that information without damning ourselves or Leonard there inside the China hub."

"That, and Strand played to Leonard's hand without even knowing it," she adds.

"Well, it doesn't hurt for our boy to amass more wealth and property, especially at times like this when we'll have to pull up stakes again, I'm sure," Wizard says with a shrug. "But you know, that's always been the way with him."

"So, once we extract him, we expose all of the board's dirty laundry over the social media platforms, right?" she continues.

"Yes, mistress. Or what's left of the platforms anyway," he responds. "There's already trouble in the Chinese board, based on the radio buzz."

"I'm 100 percent sure Strand is behind any trouble we're seeing with China," she responds.

As Cy finishes her breakfast, Wizard lifts one of her legs and sets her ankle on his knee, rotating her foot gently as part of her therapy.

"Feeling a faint little prickle, like cold feet in hot water, at the toes," she says. "That's good, right?"

"A sign your nerves are reconnecting, yes!" he answers, brightening for a second. "Now, back to our issue at hand. If Mane is caught, we will have to worry about him exposing our location and those of the other clans around here. I mean, Mane ... He's never had much loyalty to our cause. If caught, he will not suffer torture well. And he loves Allure too much to wipe his memory."

"Allure is exactly why he wouldn't talk—because she is here, and he wouldn't want her hurt," Cy responds. "In fact, I think we should send her to DC to get them all the hell out of there before it's too late."

"Are you sure?" Wizard asks, concerned. "She's our only muscle now."

"She'll go anyway," Cy answers. "And we have R3x, our Wi-Fi sensors, our cameras, our panic doors, and the boys. Between Adam's skills with drones and Michael's sharpshooting, we should be fine. So, let's help Allure help Mane. It's the least we can do."

Thirty minutes later, Allure joins Cy at the computer workroom after making it there in record time.

"Where's R3x?" Allure asks as she enters. "He wasn't in the usual spot upstairs."

"He's with the kids in the bomb shelter. They had a late night apparently," says Cy, who's 3D mapping locations between GlobeCom's DC hub and the Watergate.

"So, I see where you're mapping to," Allure observes. "Is this because you know that Mane went with Skew to DC?"

"Well, he left without telling anybody, but we think so," Cy answers. "And we have a plan. Can we talk outside? I need some air."

Once in the fresh air on the ramp, Cy takes a deep breath, trying to center, and Allure follows along with a deep breath of her own. Midday sunlight filters in and out between the foliage as they quietly navigate the wheelchair down a wooded path toward the bomb shelter.

"Wizard and I think you should lead an extraction team as soon as possible," Cy says after a moment. "We will provide all resources we can."

Allure pauses next to Cy who stops her wheelchair and looks up to meet her eyes. They are enveloped in beams of light piercing the canopy.

"What is this *really* about, Cy?" Allure asks suspiciously. "You've never seemed so happy to send me into battle and give me extra resources."

"You're right," Cy says, pausing a second to collect her thoughts. "I've had to keep a very large secret from you, my dearest, most trusted friend."

"You know I don't like being buttered up. Just tell me what you need to tell me," Allure says.

"It was for your own safety and the safety of the clans," Cy continues.

"Don't ask, don't tell," Allure interrupts. "Yada, yada. Only those with a need to know ..."

"Well, now you need to know," Cy says, pausing again to form the right words. "The man they are going after in DC, Leonard Smith, is actually our mole. He's one and the same as d_ArkAngl, and he's been helping our cause all along. Now he—and the clan members going after them—are in great danger from other, larger forces who are after Leonard."

Allure is momentarily at a loss for words, giving Cy a window to tell more of the story.

"Before I married or even met Des, I was secretly joined to Leonard, and we are still bound at the heart," Cy hastily continues. "He's been supporting us this entire time, along with Wizard, who's like a father to him."

"Am I hearing right?" Allure asks, incredulous. "You've been with Leonard Smith, who's our mole d_ArkAngl, this whole time? As a lover? And Wizard is *rich*? No way. I find that hard to believe."

"Wizard used to work with Leonard until Leonard was caught by DoD. They're both experts at acquiring assets and holdings—like this ridge, for example ..." Cy explains, trailing off.

Allure is still unbelieving, especially since they just buried Des, Cy's other husband.

"Did Des know?" Allure asks.

"Des and Leonard knew about one another, yes, but they didn't know each other personally. Leonard actually had him vetted and sent here as my protection. I'm guessing by Des's good looks, Leonard was thinking about more than just protection for me in the long-term plan. Eventually, Leonard also had to marry to keep up appearances—just as Des and I did."

"Yes, we know, Leonard Smith is married to Ying Liu. We all know who she is and who her mother and family are," Allure answers. "So, did you even love Des?"

"Oh my God, I love Des still—with all my heart. But in a different way than how I love Leonard," Cy responds. "I never think about the one when I'm with the other. And I don't see Leonard very often. The last time was a year ago."

Allure's wheels are turning as she makes the connections.

"Adam? Um ... Is Leonard Adam's father?" Allure asks. "I ask because Adam doesn't look at all like Des."

"Des was a true father to both of the boys. But, to your question, yes, Adam is Leonard's biological son," Cy confesses.

"So, Michael is Des's biological son? I'm guessing because they look so much alike," Allure surmises.

Cy nods, silent for a moment as Allure digests it. Then Alure grows angry again.

"Why did you not tell us this last night when we *did* have a need to know, when Skew brought up the plan?" she accuses.

Cy fidgets and pushes her chair forward a little, but Allure stops the wheelchair and holds Cy in place, looking in her eyes for the answer.

"I, uh, Wizard and I ... We needed to first get a message to Leonard to divert him from the Watergate, which isn't easy with the GlobeCom backbone down. Secondly, who and how many of the clan members do we tell? And we did plan to get Skew alone and tell him this morning. We didn't expect that anyone would be leaving in the night."

At this, Allure blows up. "So now, the man *I* love is out there going after one of the good guys, but who they think is a bad guy, with other, worse bad guys after all of them. Do I have it right?" Allure asks sarcastically. "And let's not forget, my man's a wuss, unable to protect himself like your Des could."

Cy fights back tears as she nods in agreement with everything Allure is saying.

"I know you're going after Mane whether anyone thinks it is a good idea or not," Cy offers. "And you are the best one for a job like this. So please, take the tools that you want. Our best resources are at your disposal."

Allure is quiet as she forms a plan. When she speaks again, she is resolute. "You're damn right I'll take the resources I need," Allure says. "I need to bring Adam. And R3x."

ONE YEAR EARLIER

"Wouldn't it be great if R3x could shoot lasers from his eyes?" Adam asked Michael as they tinkered with R3x's interface in the workroom. "I mean, he could kill people and cut through walls and stuff. I've been working out the specs."

"It'd take a lot of juice to support that type of charge," Michael responded.

"I know. I've been working on that with Dad. Diamond crystal nuclear batteries—the ones he uses in the drones should work," Adam said excitedly. "By the way, what are you doing with R3x right now?"

"Programming him to speak and interpret multiple languages," Michael answered.

"Bark!" said R3x, as if in agreement.

"Good boy," Michael said as he made one more adjustment. "Let's try his English Butler language."

"Hello, R3x!" Adam said, sitting down on the work stool next to Michael.

"Hello, young master, Adam," R3x responded with a mechanical-sounding British accent.

"He still sounds like an AI," Adam said.

"I know, I know. It's his worst voice. I was trying to adjust it," Michael agreed. "Listen to this instead."

"Hola!" Michael said to the little dog as it wagged its stubbly tail.

"Buenos dias, senior Michael," R3x responded in nearly perfect diction and accent.

"His Spanish accent sounds more real than his English voice," Adam said with a chuckle.

"Yeah, that one was easy to upload," Michael agreed.

Changing the subject, Adam asked, "Hey, um, are you going to the rave at Auntie Allure's tonight?"

"I don't think so," Michael answered. "I mean, it's probably going to be full of old people and some of them go into that S&M room downstairs. Gross, if you ask me."

"Hey! Forty-something isn't over the hill, you know," interrupted Cy who'd just got in from a run and caught their conversation as she was passing the workroom. "I just ran seven miles, and I'm not dying any time soon."

"Oh. Hi, Mom," the boys said in unison.

"We didn't see you there," Michael added.

"How was your ridge run?" Adam asked.

"It was beautiful as always—but hot," she answered, her skin gleaming with sweat. "I passed by Mane and Allure's place on the way back. Looks like Mane outdid himself on the audiovisuals this year."

"I hear a couple of outside clans are coming," Adam noted.

"Yes, and Saoirse will be there too. She's already on the way with her brothers and her father," Cy responded.

"Oh," Adam answered. "I've got to figure out what to wear."

"Green would look nice with your coloring. And it matches Saoirse's incredible eyes," she teased.

Adam flushed as Michael and Cy had a little laugh at his expense.

"Oh, and since you're working on old R3x there, that dog's hair really needs replacing," Cy said, changing subjects. "He's dirty, matting, and balding in the places where everyone pets him and picks him up. Do you think you can freshen him up?"

"Well, we hadn't thought about that," said Michael, realizing his mom was right. "But Adam's been thinking about giving him laser eyes."

"And a laser butt," Adam said, pleased with himself. "I think he should shoot out both sides."

⬤⬤⬤

Eight hours later, just after midnight, Adam and Michael arrived together at the rave. Michael was dressed in black jeans and a gray muscle shirt with the letters UFJ and an image of a hand flipping the birdie in rainbow colors on front and back. Adam went all out for this party, spiking his strawberry-blond hair into three points on top and shaving the sides bald. He was dressed in a fitted black T-shirt and jeans, finished with an emerald-green cummerbund.

Allure, with her stilettos, towered over everyone coming and going from the entrance. Trance music played in sync with blinking lights flashing through a crack in the curtain behind her. When Adam and Michael approached her table at the entrance, she looked delighted to see them.

"Boys! I wasn't sure you would come, but I'm glad you did!" she said. "The other young people will be glad you're here too."

"Hi, Auntie," they both said in unison.

She was dressed in her signature sleeveless vinyl unitard, this one bloodred with a black velvet corset that flattened her already small breasts. She finished the outfit with a matching black velvet choker dangling a small, bloodred padlock (in the locked position). A matching feathered mask with black rhinestones around the eyes pulled her whole look together.

"Welcome to our abode," she continued. "Note that a couple of things are off limits—like the moonshine—you're too young, and your parents would kill me. And the pot, which is not good for young, forming brains, and we've told Wizard to keep you away from that shit, including the edibles. Oh, and the playroom downstairs is twenty-one years and older; a key is required, and the guard at the door has been instructed on who is *not* allowed in. Neither of you are allowed in."

"Like we'd want to see any of that shit anyway," said Michael with a twisted grin. "Bunch of old people going at it like a pack of dogs."

Ignoring him, Allure continued, "Oh, and you each need a mask. Made these myself. Let me see …"

She picked out a deep-green, feathered mask to match Adam's colors and a brilliant burgundy mask for Michael.

"Are your parents coming?" she asked.

"No," said Michael. "I think they're looking forward to a night alone."

To which, Adam wrinkled his nose and replied, "TMI!"

"OK, well, have fun. Party goes all night. We've got sleeping cots in the shed if you get tired and don't want to walk home," she added. "Please stay hydrated. There are spring water stations all over the place. Oh, and we have some new youth coming from Ashville. They should be here momentarily."

She pulled apart two thick velvet blankets acting as curtains for the door, and the boys stepped into the flashing strobes.

The tent was thumping with techno trance music as a sea of people mostly dressed in black undulated with the rhythm. Mane was at the controls in the front-right corner of the tent, his cane leaning against the console. He was wearing his golden embroidered silk vest, black tuxedo pants, burgundy cape, and top hat. He wore no shirt under the ensemble, so curly light-red hairs poked above the V of his vest and out the armpits.

As the boys scanned the scene, Saoirse, fifteen, sauntered up between them from behind.

"Hello, boys!" she said, putting a hand on each of their elbows.

It'd been a while since they'd seen her, and in that time, her small, boyish figure had grown curves, a true hourglass, which she highlighted with a deep V-cut golden-green gown and black-and-green plaid corset. The corset was also equipped with small gossamer fairy wings attached to the back that she flapped with a manual pull stick at her side. Her mask matched the wings, which picked up the greens and golds in her outfit and her eyes.

Adam, gobsmacked, couldn't muster his words, so Michael stepped in first, wrapping Saoirse in a big brotherly hug and lifting her off the ground.

"Saoirse! So good to see you," Michael said as he put her down. "Are your brothers here? Your dad?"

"They are," she said with a giggle. "All of them are around here somewhere."

Adam finally found his voice.

"It's only been like eight months," Adam said, clasping both her hands in his. "And, I mean, you look so grown-up. Really, *really* great."

At that, she blushed, and Michael realized it was time to take his leave.

"I need to find Elven," Michal said. "I'm going to see if he can help us with the power requirements for supporting the new lasers in R3x."

After an awkward moment of silence, Saoirse finally spoke. "How is little R3x anyway?" she asked. "And what's this about lasers?"

"R3x can speak now—in ten languages," Adam said excitedly. "But … I think we can give him the ability to actually k-i-l-l something with lasers … I'm actually working out the power requirements for that now."

Adam realized he was talking too fast and using the word *actually* too much, so he abruptly changed course. "Um, do you need something to drink? I know I can use some water."

"I think I know just the place," Saoirse responded, taking him by the hand and leading him out of the tent.

The drinking station included a little homemade bar built around the trunk of a living tree with mugs hanging from its branches. They used a handpump next to the arrangement to draw water from a spring through a filter and fill their mugs. They were finishing their first mug of water when Michael returned, excited and flustered.

"Guys! Guys! You've got to see this! I was trying to find Elven, and I just saw something that I can't unsee," he said breathlessly. "He … Elven, went to the S&M room!"

"Oh yeah, Elven's twenty-one now. But I didn't think he'd actually go through with it," Saoirse responded, surprised.

"Oh, he's down there all right. I saw him go in with a leash in hand, like he was looking to be the dom," Michael continued. "But that's not all of it. There's something else you've got to see. C'mon! Follow me …"

The three of them reached the little shack behind the tent and entered casually. Inside, it was decorated like a sultan's tent with silk pillows for lounging tossed casually around Eastern-influenced area rugs.

They approached the door to the stairs leading to the below-ground playroom.

"OK, OK, so at the entrance, there's this guard; that's the part I can't unsee," Michael said as they approached the door. "Look at him and tell me what *you* think."

The three of them casually walked past and inspected the wisp standing at the top of the staircase—a rail-thin, twenty-something, androgynous humanoid asking any adult passerby to take them downstairs and do as they will. The wisp wore nothing but a velvet choker (no lock) and a silky pair of hot pink women's panties—beneath which stood an impressive erection.

"Oh gawd, oh gawd! Why'd you show me that?" Saoirse said as they ran outside, falling on the soft grassy ground. "That was so bad. Now *I* can't unsee it."

A few hours later, the three of them ended up in the computer workroom, with Cy and Des fast asleep in their bedroom down the hall.

Saoirse was kicking Michael's and Adam's asses in the wall of sheep. She found, connected, and then isolated more of the GlobeCom data center backup locations than the two brothers combined. Her score on the overhead with the gold icons showed her as the lion and shamed Adam and Michael who were listed as sheep.

After a while, Adam stood and stretched his arms over his head, his pants slipping down revealing a pale hip.

He looked at Saoirse. "Aaaah I need to stretch. And pee. Definitely need to pee. Then I'm heading outside for a breath of air."

Saoirse, engrossed in her work, didn't get the hint. So, Adam tried again.

"It's a full moon tonight ... Should be nice out there," he said, louder.

This time, Saoirse looked up and winked at Adam to acknowledge she'd be following him up in a bit.

Outside, the full moon was setting behind the canopy, and Adam needed to howl, hopefully with Saoirse. He waited. And waited. He did fifty jumping jacks and dropped into fifty push-ups. He stretched his calves and touched his toes. Still no Saoirse. Then he began thinking maybe something exciting was going on in the simulation without him. Maybe she and Michael unlocked a bunch of vulnerabilities and unleashed exploits while Adam's name was being smeared all over the wall of sheep.

So, Adam jogged back in, past R3x, and down the staircase. After stopping in the kitchen to grab two Yerba mates, he sauntered back into the lab, stopping in his tracks when he saw Saoirse wrapped in Michael's strong and manly arms.

"Really?" he asked, slamming the glass jars so hard on a table they nearly broke. "My brother. Why? Because he's so much more muscled and taller than I am?"

"Oh," said Saoirse, pulling away from Michael and realizing what this must look like. "This isn't what it seems. Your brother ... Michael ... He was just opening up to me about something important."

"I ... I can see that," Adam responded sarcastically. "And you are opening up to him, too—like ... like a flower, I see. While I waited under a full moon. Alone ..."

"Adam, that's not what I meant," Saoirse said as Adam stormed out.

Saoirse tried to go after Adam, but Michael stopped her.

"Leave him," Michael said, stoically. "He'll get over it. And he'll be back to complete the simulation."

"That's cold," she shot back. "He's jealous of you, you know. It would help him get over that if you tell him what you just told me."

"If he can't figure it out himself, then why should I bother?" Michael shrugged indifferently.

"You need to go after him," Saoirse pleaded.

"He'll cool off," Michael said while continuing the simulation.

Saoirse unleashed a string of angry profanities at him and Adam, mostly in Irish.

"You're an ass," she said finally as she packed up her things to go sleep at Allure's. "You're both asses. I don't want anything more to do with either one of you."

CHAPTER 11.

BATTLE FOR THE CSOS

PRESENT DAY

As the ultrasonic taxies toward the private takeoff runway at Beijing's Daxing Airport, Leonard Smith has no idea what's in store for him in DC. But he suspects foul play is at work.

He sips from his glass of Dom and downs another jumbo shrimp, looking like a man with no cares in the world. Internally, however, he feels like he's savoring his last meal. And all he can think about is Ying. He still hasn't heard from her *or* her family for more than twenty-four hours.

"Very unlike her," he says to himself as he scrolls through their images in his VAGs. "And nothing from your mother and sisters, who are usually calling me ten times a day ..."

Leonard looks at an image of their wedding party with all eight bridesmaids surrounded by Ying's family—the image so large that he has to scroll three times to get to the end of it. He takes a long sip of his champagne, thinking. Something else is at play here, but what? And by whom? And how is Ying's departure and his trip to DC a part of it?

He hasn't slept all night, and he's exhausted from thinking. So, he removes his VAGs, powers them down, and tells the cabin controls to switch to sleep mode. As soon as the lights dim and his seat reclines, Leonard is fast asleep.

Two hours later, as the plane touches down in Dulles, a soft dinging sound emanates from his mother-of-pearl cufflink, which is actually a tiny data receiver that turned on when it came in range of land-based signal towers. Given this was his ultraprivate frequency, he realizes the message has to be from Wizard.

Leonard pulls out his personal VAGs, which are rigged with a pin-size port, and plugs the cufflink directly into the miniature port. The one new message waiting reads:

Title: Travel Advisory for Those en Route
Message: Watch for long layovers; all hubs impacted, including inbound and outbound

Layover is their code word for the Watergate, and *hubs* refers to each of the three GlobeCom hubs (China, Americas, Euro-Arab). The term *inbound and outbound visitors* means that people are coming after him from all sides.

The only promising wording is *en route*.

"Good," Leonard says to himself. "At least I get to see Bossa again."

The message self-deletes, and he replaces his cufflink. He now knows that his hunch is right. Leonard's been ordered to attend this meeting in the DC central office under threat from God knows who's left of the GlobeCom leadership structure. Yet, he's going because he needs to keep up appearances that he is doing his job, attending his meeting as scheduled, and being the team player. Also, he can't resist this last opportunity to wreak a little more havoc on the remnants of GlobeCom and its board if he gets the chance while in the DC hub.

Leonard looks out the window to the private runway strip, which is clean and eerily empty. Then he looks toward the commercial runways, where unused planes are parked side by side all the way up to the empty terminals. It appears that only one runway is operational for essential travel.

Good choice not to fly commercial, he thinks.

As he disembarks, Leonard half-expects armed goons to be waiting for him. Instead, he gets through the empty private plane lobby without problems. But instead of exiting out front where his GlobeCom pickup is waiting, he decides to walk through the public terminal, which has only a handful of commercial travelers moving about. Keeping his eyes down and facing away from cameras, he hops into a smart cab at curbside and directs it to drive toward GlobeCom's DC hub.

The cab navigates by using its own cameras, matching up with local sensors and relying on its stored maps. As it exits the 395 to New York Avenue, a hoard of emergency vehicles races up behind him. The cab pulls over and waits as they pass by, one after another: an ambulance, then two more, and fire trucks, followed by at least a dozen local police and SWAT vehicles. As they pass him, Leonard gets a sick feeling in his stomach.

"Slow to five miles per hour," he directs the cab as it passes through the roundabout connecting New York Avenue to Massachusetts Avenue.

A block down the road at the 1201 building is the US cyberheadquarters for GlobeCom, staffed with its most strategic IT and infosec professionals and outfitted with state-of-the-art security technology. The scene out front is chaos—emergency vehicles, lights flashing, and police with weapons drawn running into the building.

"Change of route," Leonard says to the smart cab. "Drop me at the National Museum of Women in the Arts across the street."

The cab makes a sharp left and turns down a small side street, dropping him on the corner. He lets the cab go and steps back into the shadowy arches in the historic women's museum building, so he's out of view of cameras. He removes a small observation drone from his pull case, powers it up, and switches it to stealth mode, which renders the drone silent and invisible.

Slowly, patiently, d_ArkAngl guides his invisible drone over the emergency vehicles, past the yellow crime scene tape, and through the open double doors in front of the GlobeCom building. Then, he lags the drone above and behind the first responders up the emergency stairs to floor number three.

When the drone reaches the third-floor lobby, Leonard sees carnage everywhere. The automated reception station had been blown to bits, along with the cameras monitoring it and the weapon turrets protecting it. Biometric access controls at the door were rendered useless because the door was cut apart with a laser knife.

He steers the drone behind the response team to the conference room where he is supposed to be meeting with Ron Meeker's group at this very moment. An armed responder steps in first, gun pointed, and looks around.

"This one's cleared," he says after a few seconds. "No survivors."

With shaky hands, Leonard steers the drone into the conference room after the responders move on.

The room is eerily quiet but for the clicking and bleeping of computing devices left on during the commotion. The comm lines are open, and the overhead screens are still scrolling global damage and vulnerability reports on a 3D map of the GlobeCom network.

Leonard doesn't want to do it, but he must. Slowly, he points the drone cameras down toward the conference table.

What he sees causes him to gasp and step back farther into the alcove, where he bumps his head against an arched stone doorjamb.

He looks at the image again and sees Ron Meeker splayed half on, half off the conference table, his suit and tie soaked with dark blood. His VAGs are still attached and blinking. Leonard also recognizes two more young technicians from among the half dozen bodies slumped and bloody on the floor.

"Dear young Myra, the most brilliant among our developers," he mumbles.

He wants to scream, hurl, and punch something all at the same time.

Leonard then realizes Ron's goggles are still recording, so he wirelessly connects his drone memory to a virtual port in Ron's VAGs and downloads the entire cache of image and audio data. Then, he stealthily directs his drone back to him.

"Time to make myself scarce," he says as he repacks the drone in his case.

Still in the shadows, he removes his jacket and tie, stuffing them in his pull case, and replaces them with a blue pullover sweater and a Washington football team cap. Then, he jerry-rigs the exit door to open behind him and slips into the Women's Museum.

In a private stall in the bathroom, he messages the Global twenty-four and their security details, attaching the files he uploaded from Ron Meeker's VAGs. With comms down, some of these messages will get through, and others won't, but he's betting enough of them will get through to do the job of sewing anarchy among the board members.

"I'm uploading video from Ron Meeker's visual aid goggles," he dictates to the message group, solemnly. "This footage was taken at the DC hub, the date and time stamps are real. If you are getting this message, it means I am either dead or will be soon.

I'm also sending some damning data that may lead you to who orchestrated this bloodbath at the DC hub."

He uploads several terabytes of data on GlobeCom's dirty board members, including their families and associations, their location data, assets, passcodes, and anything else that could be used to help the board members annihilate each other. He leaves out Adrianna Dupres, who evidenced no culpability except as an unwitting pawn. He also doesn't upload the damning data he'd collected on Ying's esteemed mother from the China hub, out of loyalty to Ying and her family.

Leonard ends his message by adding, "You will also see that Damian Strand is not who he says he is."

After sending the message, he inserts a pair of brown-colored eye contacts with fake retinas to confuse the scanners. Then, he pulls up his left sleeve and points a pen-like extractor into the skin of his forearm just above the wrist.

"This is going to hurt," he says.

He clicks a button on the device, and the extractor sucks out his UI, at the same frying the chip's circuits and cauterizing his wound, leaving the faint smell of burning skin.

He flushes the fried chip and washes up, looking at himself in the mirror for a moment.

"Goodbye, Leonard Smith," he says under his breath. "Now I'm just d_ArkAngl."

Meanwhile, back at the UFJ home base, Cy and Michael are packing up for a hasty evacuation.

"I'm not sure what to put in the bag for Adam," Michael shouts from the room that he shares with Adam, which is across the hall from Cy's room. "I hope I don't miss his most important things that I don't know about."

"Do your best," Cy hollers from her room, distracted with her own packing. "And don't tell me if you find anything I shouldn't know about."

Thunder rumbles overhead, and Cy pauses to listen. "The caves are going to flood again if it doesn't stop raining soon," she observes.

"Wizard said his cave has already flooded. He opened the door and let the water in on purpose," Michael shouts from his room. "We can't carry out all of our electronics and expect them to fit on the plane. And he doesn't trust that EMPs alone will be enough to destroy all evidence."

"I see, I see. So, we fry what we can and let the water do the rest," she repeats. "Genius! And just a little bit evil, like your dad."

"Thank you! Wizard and I thought of it together," Michael beams.

Cy drags a duffle with her jewels and gold into the hallway and drops it unceremoniously on the stone floor. Piled all around her are boxes and baskets, bins and suitcases ready for a ride up the dumbwaiter to Wizard's waiting truck.

"Mom, whatever that is, it sounded heavy," Michael shouts, still shoving things into his and Adam's duffle bags. "Aren't we supposed to limit the weight?"

"Yes, but we will need the valuables for trade now more than ever," she answers, looking guiltily at the four gold bars she has stacked by the lift, 110 pounds of weight give or take a few ounces. "The plane can seat six with luggage, so we should be OK since there will only be four of us."

"Right, but don't forget, Wizard's bringing the chickens, and we can't leave our goat to the bears, so Bessie's coming too," he argues.

Michael pulls his last two duffle bags into the hallway and looks around, hands on hips. "*Mom, this is a lot of shit to carry out* to Wizard's truck. He's too old and too tired to help me anymore," he says. "And we need to get a move on."

Just like his father, Cy thinks, as she opens a drawer and puts her whole face in it to smell Des this one last time. She takes out one of his worn muscle shirts and pulls it on over her sport bra. She's still wearing sweats and his moccasins because they are easy and flexible as she learns to dress herself again. She reaches for her deerskin jacket and places it across her lap.

"Goodbye, Des. Goodbye, home that we raised the boys in," she whispers to herself in her antique round mirror.

Then she opens a velvet box on the dressing table and dons her black pearl necklace, adding, "Hello, our next life ..."

ONE YEAR EARLIER

Cy was in the workroom, scrolling through her latest dump of inmate data on her big screen, trying to find anyone who resembled Bilbo.

"Are you guys ready yet?" she hollered out the open door to the kitchen. "I need help searching through these entry logs and images."

At Cy's call, Adam and Michael skidded into the workroom like they were just in a footrace.

"Sorry, Mom," Michael said, as he squeezed in before Adam. "What were you saying?"

"Do you have any idea how many people they've stashed in the camps?" she asked, exasperated. "There are literally tens of thousands on this new list, and at least half of them are unidentified ..."

"So, are you still trying to find Bilbo? Hasn't it been like ten years?" asked Adam.

"It's been nine years, actually—to the day," Cy answered. "Today is the anniversary of when Bilbo went out on a food-and-supply run and never returned."

"So why are we still wasting time with that?" Michael asked a little coldly. "He's either working in a camp or dead. Either way, we'll never find him."

"I can't believe you *said* that, let alone think that!" Cy responded angrily. "Of course we'd still be searching for Bilbo, especially on this anniversary. He was like family. Now sit yourself down and help."

Michael and Adam grudgingly took the stools next to her and pulled up the files.

"These are about two weeks old," Adam said as he opened a roster for Camp 24 in South Africa. "People come and go from this camp all the time, and most leave dead from the heat and disease."

"If Bilbo *is* alive, though, do you think he remembers anything yet?" Michael asked.

"I doubt it. The brain wipe should last a decade or more," Cy answered.

"Although it shouldn't erase his natural inclinations," Michael added. "Like his thing for bare feet."

"Right, my son," she answered. "Bilbo's work ethic and technical inclinations would make him valuable to the work camps. That's why I'm convinced he's still alive."

"Why do you think the chipped people put up with all their friends and family members disappearing to the camps?" Adam asked. "I mean, don't these people have loved ones?"

"Usually, they just brand the disappeared as outlaws, saying they did something really bad like kiddie porn or murder—things nobody in their right mind wants to be associated with," Michael answered. "And people believe it because how could GlobeCom be wrong?"

"Michael's right," Cy acknowledged. "It's a game of smoke and mirrors, and because they own the data and the social platforms, well, they can make people believe almost anything they want."

CHAPTER 12.

POWER GRAB

PRESENT DAY

Damian and Adrianna are snuggling in an ornate, gold-trimmed bed, a view of the Eiffel Tower lit up in the distance. They'd just made love, and Adrianna feels warm and satiated. Damian is sitting up against the headboard, tracing small, circular motions around Adrianna's temples as she lounges against his chest, wrapped up in his legs, her back to him. He rubs her shoulders, massages her neck, and kisses the back of her head, familiarly, tenderly.

"Who would have believed we would still be together after all of this?" she purrs. "Adrianna Dupres and Damian Strand ..."

Without warning, he grabs a firm hold of both sides of her head and snaps her neck, killing her efficiently and mercifully—before she has time to realize (let alone fear) her impending demise.

"Sorry, my love. It's Strandeski, not Strand. And you never really did know me," he says sadly, as Adrianna's light drains from the room. "I loved you ... in my own way. But I owe my loyalty to mother Russia. Not you, not France, and certainly *not* the fucking EU."

Back in DC, d_ArkAngl feels his only choice is to go to the Watergate and head off all this madness with the clans. Getting there on foot isn't easy, but walking is his safest option. He's holding up an umbrella to fend off the rain while pulling an overnight case up and down steep, slippery sidewalks. He is mostly numb, processing what he just saw through his drone.

He crosses through George Washinton University campus just as the rain stops, the clouds break, and the sun's rays suddenly warm his skin. But he barely notices. Through his mind's eye, he keeps repeating the image of Ron's body sprawled out on the conference table.

Ron Meeker. What did he ever do to deserve this? He had a family, two kids, a wife, and a dog. He paid his taxes. He did his job, day after day, which was thankless and demanding and kept him awake at night. Ron Meeker wouldn't hurt a fly.

d_ArkAngl feels a growing rage as he keeps right to merge onto the Potomac Parkway walking path. Just then, three army helicopters fly in formation over the river, rays of sun making haloes around their spinning blades. He stops to look up, always in awe when he sees them pass over that way.

"Hopefully, you're going after the fuckin' assholes who killed Ron," he says under his breath.

With the rain passed, small boats and kayaks are back out on the waterway. Leonard stops a moment to mix in with people at the river railing so he can scan the crowds for Allure, who shouldn't be hard to spot based on Cy's description.

It doesn't take long to find Allure, sitting at an outside table at the Kingbird Café, where she is covertly scanning the crowd with her chip reader, looking for Leonard Smith's unique identifier. She's sipping a latte with a tray of sweets in front her and a redhead teenage girl across from her enthusiastically devouring the goodies.

d_ArkAngl takes the table close behind Allure's, so he can hear their conversation. They are talking in hushed tones, but he gets most of what they're saying. They're looking for someone, and he realizes it's their own team members. They're trying to stop them from doing something stupid.

He scoots backward in his small metal bistro chair so that it's almost touching Allure's, back-to-back.

"Don't turn around," he says. "I'm a friend of Cy's. She's told me all about you, Allure. Thanks for being so good to her."

Saoirse, looking suddenly panicked, is about to speak when Allure shushes her.

"Keep your eyes on the sweets, girl. And act like you're talking with me and me alone," Allure advises.

As Saoirse puts on her best jabbering act, Allure asks the man behind her to prove himself. "Tell me something about Cy that nobody knows," she demands.

"I know she's petrified of snakes but lives in an area where snakes are plentiful," he says. "I know she lives under the ground. Oh, and by the way, how's Adam?"

"OK, I'm listening."

"I've booked room 624, name of Stewart. Meet me there in thirty minutes," he says, standing to leave. "I have to show you something. And I need to know how Cy is."

To ease his mind, Allure offers him a bone. "I can tell you, Cy's safe."

"Thanks," he says as he rises to leave. "I needed to hear that."

Across the world at Work Camp 74, Ying is being processed in a sterile room with white cinder block walls. She is still wearing the same clothes she had on when Adrianna's guards snatched her—stylish black boots, leggings, and an oversized white blouse with a calf-length black wool designer coat. She's strapped to a worn-looking exam table, the back raised so she is sitting up. Two guards stand at the door watching as a tired-looking female doctor in her fifties turns on her pen light.

"Single female, local data on her UI says she is forty-five, from Boston, mixed race, name of Bao Reese," says one of the guards in a strong Russian accent.

"I'm not forty-five. I'm forty-two," says Ying, confused.

"Please follow my fingers with your eyes," instructs the doctor with an accent that is distinctly Midwestern United States.

"You speak English?" Ying asks as her eyes follow the light. "I ... I demand to be released. My family will not tolerate this."

The doctor doesn't respond, instead focusing on Ying's evaluation.

"I don't belong here. I am Ying Liu, daughter of the Chinese director of the board!" Ying continues. "Check my UI."

"We did check your identity data, and it says you are Bao Reese, not Ying whoever you say you are," says the other guard at the door, who's also American.

"Then they switched the data in my UI!" Ying argues.

"Impossible," the Russian guard responds. "Zee UIs, they are unhackable."

"Of course, the chips are Chinese tech ... Just saying," the American guard interjects.

"Look us up on the social platforms. There are pictures of us all over the place," Ying pleads. "News of our wedding, of our careers—it's all there."

The doctor steps back and tucks the light pen back into the chest pocket of her lab coat.

"They warned us that you'd say something like that also, which is convenient given the social platforms are down," the doctor responds. "Listen. You're all mixed up because you hit your head—although scans show no sign of concussion."

Ying, confused, reaches for her head and feels a tender lump just above her right temple.

"*They* did this to me! Adrianna Dupres and her goons did this!" Ying says. "My *brain* is just fine."

The doctor ignores her as she makes another note on her digital pad.

"It's a conspiracy, I tell you. My husband—he's Leonard Smith, CSO for the China hub," Ying continues.

"This one's cleared to move," the doctor says, directing the guards at the door. "Take her to section two to test her skills."

Then, to Ying, she adds, "What are you good at, my dear?"

"I'm … I'm in stocks and finance," Ying answers, confused. "So, I'm good at numbers and predictions, I suppose. Why?"

The doctor makes another note in her file, and the guards lead Ying down a circular-shaped hallway with cement floors. Midway down the hallway, they pass a wall of windows, giving her a wide view into a warehouse-sized space with at least three hundred people programming on 3D simulators. At the head of the room watching over all of them is a middle-aged man, short and wide-bellied, with bare feet that are as large as they are hairy. Ying meets eyes with him for a brief moment, and then she passes from his view.

ONE YEAR EARLIER

Cy floated on her back in warm spring water, her hair swishing around like a veil in a breeze. Bubbles effervesced like those in champagne from the gravely ground beneath her, tickling her skin.

It was off-hours, and she was alone in the Martha Jefferson pool, also known as the ladies' pool. She was using this moment to get centered. She looked up at the half moon through an open-air skylight at the top of a high, teepee-like ceiling and let out a huge sigh. She worried about this meeting and what it would lead to, but she was also eager to see her love.

Outside, d_ArkAngl passed a small sign that read: "Jefferson Pools, Warm Springs, Virginia: Historic site visited by Thomas Jefferson in 1819, restored in 2026. Pools close at sunset. Cameras, drones, and recording devices forbidden."

He entered the roundhouse at the Martha pool and locked the door behind him. Cy took a last deep breath to finish her meditation, and he watched her without interrupting her. Then, she stood in the chest-deep water and faced him, smiling.

"Is that Venus before me?" he asked while stripping off his clothes and dropping them on the deck.

"Is that you, my love? You look a little different," Cy observed, squinting to get a better view of his changed features from across the pool.

"Oh, that. A temporary update, eyes and hair color mostly," he explained. "Trust no one ... not even our own."

As he stepped down into the 98-degree water, d_ArkAngl never took his eyes off Cy. All the while, she returned his look of lustful admiration.

"Oh my God, I've missed you," he said, pulling her into his arms. "I've missed you so much."

He brushed a lock of her wet hair out of the way and dropped his face to kiss her, long, slow, savoring her sweetness and her smell.

"I've missed you too, my love," she said, wrapping her legs around him. "We've got fifty minutes ..."

Saying no more, the lovers locked together as if no time had ever passed between them, or maybe all time had passed, making the union even sweeter.

Forty minutes later, they were on the deck above the pool, drying each other, while Cy caught him up on family matters.

"Adam is progressing nicely," she said. "But Wizard says I coddle both the boys by not turning them loose on GlobeCom."

"Understandable. You're a mother," he responded. "But Wizard's right, you know. The boys have been cyberbattle-ready for a while."

"I know, I know, but what if they end up in the camps—or worse?" she asked.

"I'd know it, and I'd get them out of there," he answered.

"You mean like how you'd know and find our Bilbo? But I don't see that you have," Cy retorted.

"That's different. Bilbo's an unidentified—*and* he wiped his memory. Do you know how many unidentifieds they have in the camps right now?" he said, a little defensively. "I'm still looking for him, my love, but I must be careful because Strand is watching my every move."

"Yes, I do, actually, because I've been searching myself," she responded.

He leaned over to nuzzle her neck, distracting her from her thoughts.

"Mmmm, you can't keep doing that," she said, feeling warm again. "They'll be here any minute."

"The door's locked, so let them wait," he answered.

Fifteen minutes later (and five minutes late), Cy opened the double doors into the round barn. Dressed in long robes with hoods covering most of their faces, they welcomed eleven other clan leaders who were dressed similarly.

As they entered, clan leaders were given a number (two to twelve) on a small piece of paper. The participants then assembled in front of their respective numbers, which were posted on the railings to the narrow, boardwalk-like deck that surrounded the pool. Cy took position number one as the leader of the UFJ Clan, while d_ArkAngl stood to her left as number zero.

This arrangement put them in a circle facing one another but also distanced each one of them enough that, with the hoods and dim lighting, they could not recognize each other if challenged to do so.

Once the clan leaders were all positioned, d_ArkAngl began. "I understand you wanted to meet me—to prove I'm real or something," he said. "I'm real, and I'm here—at great risk to all of us. So, this had better be worth it."

He was like a rock star to the clans, and everyone excitedly started talking at once.

After a moment, Cy silenced them.

"Since it's number three who called this meeting, let him start the conversation," Cy directed.

To that, number three (Skew) began in his thick Irish accent. "So, thanks to your intel, Mr. d_ArkAngl, and all your support over the years, we've fully mapped the network backbones, primary and backup data centers, networking, and even communications and observation satellites *and* their command-and-control centers," he said respectfully. "The problem is, no matter where we penetrate and take out their systems, GlobeCom rebounds almost immediately. Not only that, GlobeCom systems emerge stronger, as if our attacks are teaching them resilience."

Clan leader number nine, a female with a deep voice, cut in. "Not to mention, the general population thinks *we're* the criminals. They turn a blind eye to the control GlobeCom has over their daily lives and to those disappearing into the work camps," she said passionately.

"Our attacks haven't been entirely fruitless," countered number twelve, a male with black skin. "We've managed to spread some fear of GlobeCom's reach and power by posting evidence of their criminal activities to the social platforms before GlobeCom removed the articles."

"And we've also sown doubt by revealing that their UIs *are* hackable," added number eleven, a female with a local accent. "But it's not enough to move the needle in favor of busting up GlobeCom's power."

"That's because the general population still thinks sticking with GlobeCom is better than the unknown," added number nine.

Number three (Skew) stepped in again. "OK, OK, so back to what we're here for. The only way we can sever GlobeCom's grip is through a coordinated, perfectly timed series of proximity attacks on every one of its data centers, backup centers, and the systems controlling the communication and spy satellites," he said. "It must happen simultaneously. Across the globe."

At that, all hell broke loose, and everyone, again, started talking at once.

Cy let the room die down a little and then raised her hand to regain control. The clan leaders fell silent.

"d_ArkAngl, what have you to say?" she asked.

"GlobeCom installations are well-armed with digital cameras and remote firepower," he said. "If those deterrents don't work, they have layers of drone responders and manned, armed vehicles."

"We know their drone tech inside and out. We've been reverse engineering their drones and their command channels for years," replied number three (Skew).

"The satellites will be the hardest," said number four, a transgender with female form and a gritty male voice. "They're still on a grid formation, meaning you'll have to bump them out of alignment or otherwise shoot them from the sky."

Number seven, an Asian male, offered a solution. "We can probably do both," he said. "We can hack into the command centers and move the higher altitude sats off-grid, make them crash into each other over a slow period of time as they orbit. We can also hit the lower orbit sats with the same ground-to-satellite lasers China used in the North Korean conflict of 2028. That will at least put an end to their observation drones."

Cy blanched. She strongly objected to the use of violence, believing that their collective intelligence and hacking skills could win the cyberwar without bloodshed.

"In all these scenarios you propose, there will be innocent collateral damage. There always is," she said. "In this case, what happens when we shut down the entire network at once? Global chaos."

"Out of chaos will come order," said several of the clan leaders at the same time.

"Then there are short-term issues we'd need to be ready for ahead of time," Cy continued. "Once we take down the network, will local systems come online fast enough to feed people and care for their medical needs? And what about transportation? Will it fail safely, or will planes fall from the sky? Then there are longer-term issues, such as, do we render their UIs useless so nobody can track and control them? Or do we keep them active for a new form of computing?"

"All good points," answered number three (Skew). "We think restoring the old infrastructure of cellular data and wireless internet would enable people to transition. So, say, the data is already at the hospital you go to regularly," he explained. "Strip away the GlobeCom cloud, and the data is still in the local systems for use and validation."

"I doubt it will be that easy," Cy warned them. "A million and one things could go wrong ..."

CHAPTER 13.

BLAME THE RUSSIANS

PRESENT DAY

Once in his room on the sixth floor, d_ArkAngl finally falls apart. He sinks to the floor in the entry. He's hyperventilating, so he holds his head between his knees. He can't shake the image of Ron Meeker, of Myra, and of all those others who were shot down at the DC hub like their lives didn't matter.

Finally, he stands, his arms and legs shaking. He steps to the sink, removes his cap, and splashes water on his face.

"Pull yourself together, man. You're a blithering mess," he says to himself.

He retrieves his case that he'd left by the door and makes his way to the loveseat in front of the large window, where he places the case on the coffee table and opens it. He's preparing the drone images for personal viewing when he hears a knock on the door.

He lets Allure and Saoirse into the room, closing the door quickly behind them.

"I've got the hallway, elevator, and stairwells in a video loop. Nobody will see you were here," he explains to them at the doorway.

They look at him dumbly, and he realizes he hasn't even introduced himself.

"Sorry to meet under such circumstances ... I'm d_ArkAngl," he explains.

It takes a moment to register, and then both ladies light up.

"Oh my gosh," says Saoirse. "*The* d_ArkAngl?"

"I'm here because you are all in danger," he continues.

"Well, we're here because the clan is in danger. And Leonard Smith is too," says Allure. "That's why we're here. To protect them all."

Allure knows that d_ArkAngl is Leonard Smith, but sworn to secrecy, she is not sharing that knowledge with Saoirse.

"Yeah, well, the clans are the least of our worries," he says. As he picks up his water glass, he needs two hands to hold it still enough to drink from it. "Something quite horrible happened at the DC headquarters. People died. Good people with families. Lives snuffed out as if they didn't matter."

He takes another sip of water and then starts rambling. "GlobeCom is already self-imploding. I didn't think it would happen this fast. But I ... I ... I was late. And on my drone, I saw. I was too late. The aftermath ... I saw Ron. I saw them all ..."

"Slow down, man," Allure interrupts. "We're having trouble following. Take a deep breath and start from the beginning."

He pauses, breathes in slowly through his nose, exhales slowly through his mouth, and repeats the breathing three times, just like Ying taught him during tough times past. As he goes through the exercise, the tremor in his hands visibly reduces. He takes another sip of water and suddenly remembers there's someone young and impressionable in the room.

"Uh. Should we be talking in front of the girl?" he asks. "And, by the way, who is she?"

"She is me, and I am Saoirse," says the petite redhead with green eyes and black nail polish. "Daughter of Skew, who's leader of the Cl0ver-S clan. And I'm a big girl. *Do* keep talking."

He looks at Allure who nods, and he proceeds with his story, still scattered.

"Right. So. Someone was sent to kill Ron Meeker and Leonard Smith, two of GlobeCom's chief security officers," he says. "And whoever it was, they succeeded. Both of them are dead now, along with Ron's close technology team. I … I don't know who else was in the building, but Ron was mowed down. I saw him from the drone …"

"It wasn't our guys!" exclaims Saoirse. "Their mission wasn't to kill anyone. They just wanted the CSOs to lift their biometrics and stuff. Besides, they've been here at the Watergate this whole time. None of ours is at the GlobeCom building."

"I don't think it was anyone from the clans," he confirms. "Clearly, these were professionals with deep resources."

"Well then who was it?" Allure asks. "Are we in danger?"

"We are very much in danger being here at the Watergate where Leonard is known to stay," he answers, honestly. "He is not confirmed dead yet. So, they may still be looking for him. And I have my suspicions as to who is after him, which this video will likely prove. If I'm right, the clans are the least of our worries."

"Except that we'll have to get them out of harm's way," adds Allure, ever the protector.

"Yes, there's that complication," he agrees.

Turning to Saoirse, he adds, "Um, do you need to use the restroom or something? This next part is going to be graphic."

"Fine. I have to go anyway," Saoirse says a little snottily as she saunters toward the bathroom. (And once she shuts the door behind her, she does go, much to her relief.)

Allure repositions herself next to him on the loveseat as he opens the footage. The video appears in a two-foot electroluminescent display that emanates from his wristband. He fast-forwards through hours of recording and then slows the frames to show the last minutes of Ron Meeker's life.

Here is what they see from the perspective of Ron Meeker's VAGs:

> One of Ron's team, Myra, twenty-eight, raises her hand from the far end of the conference table.
>
> "Yes, Myra. How may I help you?" Meeker asks.
>
> "Sir, Mr. Meeker, we are wondering when Mr. Leonard Smith would arrive," she asks in her polite Indian way. "The DevOps team's very busy, and they would need me to direct them."
>
> "He should be here momentarily. He's usually not late, but nothing's normal right now," Ron answers. "Until then, let's go over our damage and patch status."
>
> He looks at his team of six around the conference table, young to middle-aged, various races and genders, all of obvious intelligence, appearing worn but not defeated. He then switches view to an overhead display screen scrolling endless lists of vulnerabilities, damages, and incident response workflows mapped against global hot spots on the network.
>
> They hear a ruckus down the hall, and Ron looks back at his team. They all recognize the

sound of gunfire at the same time, followed by shouting and explosions.

Then the building alarms go off.

"Everyone! Take cover!" shouts Meeker as he dashes to the conference room double doors that were open for the arrival of Leonard. He closes them manually and then lifts his VAGs to expose his biometric retinal key at the door panel.

"Secure room," he says to the interface by the door.

The deadbolts lock—click, click, click— making the doors impenetrable.

Ron Meeker looks around again at the faces of his coworkers kneeling behind the conference table. They are afraid but also trusting him to get them out of this.

d_ArkAngl pauses the display for a second and looks up at Allure.

"Every room on the tech floor is reinforced with thick cinder walls and bulletproof doors that can only be locked or unlocked by classified GlobeCom employees," he tells her. "It would take equally powerful biometric access to open the door. So, they know they should be safe. And yet …"

He stops talking for a moment, while Allure is silent beside him.

"I don't think I can go on. I'm dreading what comes next," he confesses.

Allure reaches over, gently holds his wrist in her hand, and then turns the feed on again.

After successfully locking up the saferoom, Ron Meeker turns to his teammates. Their look of relief is instantly replaced by panic as the bolts unlock one at a time—unclick, unclick, unclick—and the dawning realization on all their faces is that they are about to die.

Like a bear protecting its cubs, Meeker positions himself between his staff and the door, turning to face the enemy.

The doors burst open, and he zeroes in a GlobeCom badge worn by the lead attacker before he is suddenly gunned down.

Then the image jostles wildly, in and out of focus to the sound of gunfire and screaming. The VAGs shift to a cockeyed view of the ceiling and the image remains still. There are more sounds of screaming and human bodies cracking and thudding as they land lifeless on the floor. All the while, Myra can be heard in the background praying to her Hindu gods, until hers, the last voice of them all, is finally snuffed out.

d_ArkAngl stops the feed and wipes his eyes, saying, "Myra was getting married in a month. Ying and I were going to her wedding."

He turns the feed on again.

A masked face appears for an instant over Ron's VAGs, and then an arm reaches out to remove the goggles until shouting from down the hallway interrupts him.

"Stop! Police!" they hear, followed by more gunfire.

> One of the shooters, a man with a thick
> Russian accent, is audible in the background.
> "Leave them! Ve must go. Now!"
> The masked face moves out of the picture,
> and the goggles continue recording the ceiling.

d_ArkAngl stops the feed and feels a rage as he's never felt before, burning, ready to kill.

"I *knew* it. I *knew* it!" he says too loudly. "The Russians did this. They want to take over GlobeCom—or whatever's left of it. The bastards."

"So, then, what are we going to with this information?" asks Allure.

"I've already done it," he answers, calming down a bit and looking slightly evil. "I've essentially published this video, along with the board's dirty secrets and other damning information."

"Who will read it?" Allure asks. "Because, as I recall, we took the network down, including media."

"Some of this can be transferred regionally. So now the data is out there. We just have to wait for it to spread and catch fire," he explains. "Instead of milliseconds, it may take hours or days, but the information will spread."

"OK, so turn the GlobeCom board members against each other while also turning the public against them. I like that," Allure responds, still thinking. "And what about your alter ego, Leonard Smith?"

"I sent a message with the footage that if they were seeing this, Leonard Smith is dead, and now he effectively *is* dead," he says.

Then he pulls up his sleeve to reveal a burn wound, about half an inch long, where his chip should be.

"So, no doubt you want him to stay that way," Allure observes.

"What way?" d_ArkAngl asks, a little slow.

"Dead," she answers.

"Oy! Yes, obviously. Stay dead. Nobody knows I am Leonard Smith. Keep it that way," he agrees. "It's safer for me and everyone around me if those still pulling the strings at GlobeCom think I—er, Leonard Smith—is dead."

"Don't worry. Cy swore me to secrecy, although I owe her nothing," Allure says bitterly.

He doesn't miss the dig, but he can't spare the mental bandwidth right now to ask what she means by it.

"What about Strand?" she asks.

"I have a special package of information circulating about Mr. Strand, including where and how to find the criminal syndicates—information that explicitly ties him to his handle, DarkL0rd," d_ArkAngl answers, still looking a little evil. "And that he is really Strandeski, a Russian operative."

At that moment, Saoirse emerges from the bathroom with a question.

"So, do you think the Russians will come after us?" she asks.

They both look at Saoirse dumbly for a second, worried that Saoirse overheard and made the connection that d_ArkAngl is Leonard Smith.

"Were you listening? What exactly did you hear, my dear?" he asks, accusingly.

"No, I *wasn't* listening. I had the fan on the *whole time*," Saoirse says testily. "But I couldn't help thinking … I mean, with GlobeCom so badly damaged, there's now a power vacuum. And the Russians are sneaky enough to take advantage. But they can't take on the EU, China, and the United States at the same time and expect to win, can they?"

"They may think they can, and if so, that is their weakness," he responds, impressed with her intuition. "And, by the way, how can a young person be so very insightful? Your assessment is spot on."

"History is my fave," Saoirse says. "And this type of power play happens over and over again when there's a vacuum …"

Just then, Allure turns her attention to her comm. "It's Adam," she says. "He found Mane at the diplomat suite on the top floor. It's the suite that Leonard Smith had booked but never showed up for."

"Guys," she says into her comm, "You need to get out of there. Bad dudes everywhere. Take the stairwell to the floor below ..."

At that moment, Allure, Saoirse, and d_ArkAngl hear the sound of gunfire though her comm, which they also hear coming from one floor above them. Then, through the comm, they hear cussing and rustling and a door slam, followed by Adam shouting.

"Mane's been hit!"

FOUR WEEKS EARLIER

In the weeks before the UFJ team left for Operation Backbone, Wizard started showing up for every family meal. This morning, he arrived at seven o'clock with a basket of eggs and requested a mushroom and chive scramble.

"I've got it," offered Michael, who was already in the kitchen. "I was trying to figure out what to make for breakfast anyway. Adam can help."

As the boys worked on breakfast, Wizard poured himself some coffee and joined Cy and Des at the round table, where they were already drinking their morning Joe.

"We got a message last night from d_ArkAngl," Wizard said as he sat down next to them. "He thinks he found Bilbo alive and well in Work Camp 74."

CHAPTER 14.

SAVING MANE

PRESENT DAY

Adam is in the upper stairwell talking on the comm to Allure, as Mane moans in pain.

"We're on the top floor," Adam shouts. "We've blocked the fire door with the weight of our bodies ... I'm trying to lock it from the keypad now."

Without hesitation, Allure races out of the room and down the hall toward the stairwell. With her long legs, she takes the steps two at a time, meeting up with them at the landing one floor above.

Mane and Adam are leaning against the door from the inside, a streak of deep red blood smeared across the floor. The combined weight of Adam (about one hundred and fifty pounds) and Mane (who's about four hundred pounds) is for now holding off the gunmen while Adam reprograms the controller box that he's pulled from the wall jack.

Allure drops down and assesses the damage to Mane's damaged leg, immediately applying pressure to a bloody hole that went in and out through Mane's left thigh.

"We ... We were at the elevator waiting for the lift down, when GlobeCom goons stepped out and faced us," Adam says as he finishes tinkering with the control panel. "They ... the goons ... acted like they recognized me. I ... I don't know who they were. They pointed their weapons, so I ran to the stairwell. Mane was right behind."

The deadbolts on the top and bottom of the door lock, and they hear the gunmen move away.

"Don't worry. I fucked with the elevator too. They'll never make it down that way," Adam offers.

Looking past Allure and seeing the gore, Adam feels suddenly faint.

"Adam! Stay with me here. Focus, man!" Allure commands. "They hit the femoral artery. That's why there's so much blood. We need to stop the bleeding."

Adam is still about to lose it.

"Adam! *Adam!* Give me your belt," she orders.

Adam snaps to and then can't get his belt off fast enough. He hands it to Allure, who wraps it around Mane's thigh above the wound and cinches it, pulling as tight as she can. Mane wakes up from his stupor.

"Ohhhh hoooo hhhhoho ooooowwwww my God, my God. Damnit, woman!" he hollers so loudly that his voice echoes up and down the stairwell.

Allure turns the job over to Adam.

"Pull this belt tighter ... to cut off his blood flow. Even when you can't tighten it, tighten it some more. Then cinch it even tighter."

As Adam puts his full weight into pulling on the belt, Allure tears part of Mane's large white shirt into strips to wrap the wounds.

With each tug of the belt, Mane shouts louder.

"Can we cauterize it?" Adam asks.

"We can, in theory. What were you thinking?" Allure answers.

"Well, you asked me to bring R3x," Adam notes. "His laser powers are adjustable. We could lower the strength …"

"Another good idea!" Allure says as she jams the cloth strips into Mane's wound.

"Noooo! Noooo more pain. Safe word, safe word," cries Mane, who's looking up helplessly at his beloved Allure, the woman causing him such torture.

Allure shoots Mane a withering look, which silences him.

"This all could've been avoided had you talked to me before secretly taking off with Skew of *all people*," she says as she wraps the cloth around his thigh and ties it into a knot.

Mane looks up at her sheepishly. "Yes, mistress. Sorry, mistress …" he says, slurring his words.

"Mane! Don't faint. Do you hear me?" she shouts in his face. "You're too big. We need you to help us get you down the stairs."

Mane starts swaying to one side.

"Mane! Stay awake. Sit up straight! Now, use your good leg to push yourself up the wall to a standing position. Adam and I will lift from either side of you as you stand. Do it, or face my wrath," she commands.

Mane groans weekly, "Yes, mistress."

"We need to take him to our room," she says to Adam.

"OK, wait. What? We have a room?" Adam asks.

As they move down the stairs, she asks, "You say they recognized you?"

"Yeah. Weird, huh?" Adam answers.

"Um, maybe not so weird," she replies.

They move agonizingly slowly down the stairs, doing a half-fireman's carry on each side of Mane, who's using his good leg to support what weight he can. With each hop, his leg spurts more blood, but somehow Mane manages to stay conscious and keep his weight on his good leg.

Allure opens the door to floor six and looks carefully around. "Clear. We're four doors in on the right," she says.

"I'm ... I feel sick," says Mane.

Mane is flushed and sweating. Adam and Allure are supporting him with all their might in their modified fireman's carry, as Mane leans heavily on the both of them.

"Almost there, babe," says Allure. "Stay with us."

In the room, Saoirse is ready at the door and opens it as she sees them approach.

"Oh my God, oh my God! Uncle Mane, Uncle Mane," Saoirse says over and over as they push past her and drop Mane unceremoniously on the bed.

"Breathe, child," says Allure. "We need you to clean up the blood splatter in the hallway leading to our door."

Saoirse is temporarily immobilized, her mouth agape and her eyes swelling up with tears.

"No time for that. Do as I say," Allure commands.

Saoirse hustles to the bathroom by the front door, fills the tub with cold water, and adds bucket after bucket of ice from the in-room ice maker. (She knows the value of ice-cold water for removing blood from growing up with three rough-and-tumble brothers who seemed to constantly get hurt.)

As the tub fills, Saoirse throws in half the bathroom towels and brings the rest of the towels to Allure.

Allure props several pillows under Mane's leg to raise it above his heart, and Mane mercifully passes out.

"Now we need to stop the bleeding," Allure says. "Adam?"

Adam opens R3x's case, pulls him out, and attaches him to the room's power source. At that moment, d_ArkAngl, who'd been observing quietly from out of the way on the loveseat, smiles knowingly.

"I really like what you've done with R3x. The little plaid vest with the carry handle is a nice touch," he says to Adam, who until now hadn't realized d_ArkAngl was in the room.

"Auntie?" Adam says with a puzzled look on his face. "Who is this? And how does he know R3x?"

"I'll answer that question," d_ArkAngl says. "R3x was my gift your mother—a long time ago."

"Whaaaat? You knew my mom?" Adam asks. "Who the hell are you?"

"I'm d_ArkAngl," he answers.

"OK, everyone, we can go down memory lane later," Allure interrupts. "Adam, will this laser work the way we need it to?"

"Yes, if we lower the power so that it won't cut off his leg," Adam responds. "We test it first, of course."

d_ArkAngl raises an eyebrow, impressed. "You gave him laser powers?"

"Michael and I did, with a lot of help from our father," Adam says, staying focused on the laser controller and missing the slightly stricken look on d_ArkAngl's face. "OK. Let's test on the bedside table."

Adam lines up R3x's left eye with the table's edge and fires a short orange-hot laser burst. It burns a hole the size of a quarter about a half inch deep into the hardwood, leaving it sizzling and smoking.

"OK, that's a solid wood," Allure says, looking at the hole. "It went in a half inch."

"Right. I think we're ready," Adam says. "This will be a good story for Mane when he recovers—that R3x saved his life."

He hands Allure the controller. "OK, now you try."

Allure aims the laser at the bedside table for practice, while Adam coaches her.

"You can program a target. See, line it up with the digital display using this remote," Adam instructs.

She fires, and it misses the bedside table, instead shredding part of the armchair next to it, leaving it smoking and stinking. d_ArkAngl grabs a sofa pillow and snuffs it out before the smoke alarm goes off.

"Um, Adam, maybe you should do it," Allure offers. "You have a much better aim than I do."

"Are you sure, Auntie?" Adam asks.

"I'm sure."

Adam positions R3x just so, checking the alignment on his interface and without the interface and in the interface again.

"Um, this should do it," he says.

He fires a short blast, blackening Mane's wound instantly. The stench of burning flesh overwhelms the smell of smoking chair cushion.

"The bleeding is, for now, stopped," Allure observes. "But he'll need surgery to repair that artery as soon as possible, or he could lose the leg."

"Then we need to find Med!c," Adam adds.

"He's already standing by outside the beltway," Allure says. "Now we just need to get out of here."

Looking at R3x, still plugged into the room's power source and charging up again, d_ArkAngl gets an idea.

"Adam, how hot can you program those lasers to be? And how long can they fire at full power before R3x here runs out of juice?" he asks.

"Hot enough to cut through walls and furniture and stuff … and human flesh if that's what you're asking," Adam offers. "That kind of power?"

d_ArkAngl nods affirmatively. "Yes, that kind of power."

"R3x can maintain two lasers at full strength out of both ends for about thirty seconds, give or take," Adam answers.

"That should be enough," d_ArkAngl confirms.

Saoirse returns to the room, and Adam opens the door for her. They make lingering eye contact, both of them scared, vulnerable, and out of their league. She is pushing a metal serving cart with a stack of wet towels smeared pink and red with blood. She rolls the cart into the bathroom and dumps the towels into the tub, which is still full of ice water.

"I didn't have long to work before I heard people. I got the stuff closest to our door first, and there's no trace on our doorjamb," she says loudly from the bathroom so they could hear her.

"Good thinking," Allure responds. "And thanks for finding and bringing in the cart. We'll use it to transport Mane."

"We better get a move on," Adam says worriedly. "Emergency systems are going to turn on at any time."

Just then, the building alarm sounds and evacuation orders issue from a speaker above their door: "This is not a drill. There is a public safety issue on the upper floors. All guests on all floors and in all rooms and common areas must evacuate to the front plaza immediately. Elevators will not be working, and not all stairwells will be open. Consult your evacuation map on your door and follow the lit exit signs."

d_ArkAngl steps next to the bed and raises his voice over the PA. He needs to wake Mane up for some information.

"Mane, wake up! Where are your friends?" he asks. "Mane?!"

Mane stirs, asking, "What is all that screaming?"

"It's the building alarm system," d_ArkAngl answers. "Now where are the rest of your team here at the Watergate?"

"Two others ... stationed at the entrance and side doors used by patrons. Another at the service entrance," Mane manages.

"Do they have a vehicle?" d_ArkAngl asks.

"Um, a van … Um, a food delivery truck in the employee garage. What is all that screaming?" Mane asks.

Mane fades out again, and Allure shakes him to keep him awake. "How are you and the clan members communicating with one another?" she asks.

"Mostly … line of sight …" Mane grunts. " … but Skew … has a commline to my ear."

"Shit. Why didn't you tell us that sooner?" Allure says.

Allure removes the bud from Mane's ear and hands it to Saoirse.

"You take the comm now," she instructs Saoirse. "Tell your father what's going on. Ask him to round up everyone and meet us at the service elevator entrance in the employee lot. Tell them we need a wheelchair, supersized if possible."

"On it," says Saoirse as she puts the bud in her ear and walks to the corner of the room by the windows. "Da? Da? Did you hear all that?"

d_ArkAngl takes this moment to make a call.

"Meanwhile, I've gotta get a message to Bossa," he says as he stands and heads toward the bathroom. "I'll be in here with the door shut so I can hear over the damn alarm."

"Um, who's Bossa?" asks Adam suspiciously.

"She calls herself Bossa Nova. She's always been the real boss of Wizard and me, and she's going to get us the hell out of here," he answers.

Adam looks confused as d_ArkAngl retreats into the bathroom and shuts the door.

"Adam, go ahead of us and hack the service elevator in the north hall," Allure instructs. "It'll be closed now, and we need to use it to get to the underground employee lot. We'll be right behind you."

After Adam leaves, d_ArkAngl returns from the bathroom.

"OK, everything's arranged. Once we get downstairs, you-all

take the van. Adam and I have a flight to catch," he says. "Most of the clans are relocating right now." He looks around the room, adding, "Um, where's Adam?"

"He's at the north service elevator getting it opened for us," Allure responds.

"Oh shit! I haven't got that part of the floor covered," d_ArkAngl worries. "Hang on, let me get to my program."

"But anything you do now will have to blend into the evacuation, or the guards would suspect," Allure cautions.

From the peephole, Saoirse watches a parade of people in all states of dress heading toward the emergency exit lights. The alarm is still whining obnoxiously overhead, and the automated voice is still issuing the same instructions.

"The hallway will be clear in about thirty seconds," Saoirse shouts over the noise.

"OK, so I have to run the loop on the next thirty seconds, after the hallway is clear, so the guards don't think anybody's left up here and come looking," he says. "This will just take a minute."

d_ArkAngl uses his wristband to reach out to the trojan he has hidden in the hotel's building operations network. He uploads the last sixty seconds of the coverage of empty hallways and sets it into a time loop.

"OK, now they won't see us at the service area," he says.

It takes all three of them to push the heavy cart down the hallway, its wheels digging into the carpet under Mane's weight. When they reach the elevator, Saoirse sets R3x on the floor in front of the door. She pets him lovingly, and then powers him on, his little stubby tail wagging as he builds a charge.

d_ArkAngl sends his drone down the northern hall. From the drone's perspective, he sees armed masked goons heading toward their elevator, so he turns the drone around and hauls it down to the south hall, where he sees another set of armed, masked goons coming at them.

"Shit! GlobeCom goons! In both directions. We're right smack in the middle," d_ArkAngl exclaims. "And they're not all Russian, I suspect … Yes, yes, I can hear these three are speaking Mandarin. Maybe they're here to retrieve and protect Leonard Smith. I can't tell."

As the service elevator makes its way up to their floor, Adam adjusts R3x's position to be directly in-line with the approaching goons.

"Just like flying a drone," he says. "Nobody suspects a cute little doggie."

The elevator doors open, so d_ArkAngl collects his drone, and they all step in backward, facing R3x who is standing in position in front of the elevator.

Adam issues his command. "Kill, boy! *Kill!*"

As the elevator doors close in front of them, they see R3x start firing red-hot lasers out of both ends.

They witness the rest of the mayhem through R3x's eyes, as displayed on Adam's controller. While not precise, several of R3x's shots hit their mark, slicing through limbs and torsos, furnishings and walls like a hot knife through butter.

By the time the elevator doors open at the underground employee lot, none of the goons are left standing and R3x has been blown to bits.

THREE WEEKS EARLIER

The family spent a busy yet idyllic last week together. Adam and Michael set up the team's proximity trackers, mapped their locations, and gathered food. Most importantly, they helped Des practice drone fighting.

On this Sunday morning, the whole family, and even Allure,

was out together in the glen honing their warfighting skills and tweaking their technologies.

"Dad, you've got to stop that!" Adam shouted into his audio set from where he stood at the forest's edge. "When you swing to the right of my GlobeCom drones, you are in my field, and I can see through your camouflage."

To prove his point, Adam fired a paintball dead on target, coating the side of Des's invisible drone in red so everyone could see it.

"Good one, bro!" Michael said to Adam through his ear comm.

"Oy! Damn," Des exclaimed. "You're right. I should have flanked all the way left. Let's try again"

"C'mon, boys. Don't be too hard on your father. After all, he's flying six drones at once," Cy piped in through her comm bud from her spot in the middle of the garden where no one could see her. "Allure, you're up next."

Using her display from her wrist pad, Allure drilled deeper into the programming interfaces of their stolen and reverse engineered GlobeCom drones that are still in the air, trying to take them down.

"Ready, set ..."

Allure issued a command to the controllers telling the GlobeCom drones to shut down. Suddenly, four of GlobeCom's most current battlefield versions dropped to the ground.

"Mom! How'd she *do* that? I literally just installed yesterday's newest GlobeCom mobile firewall tech to protect the drone interfaces before we started this simulation," Michael said, surprised.

"What can I say? Allure's on it," Cy responded.

To which, Allure added, "Secret sauce, kids. Will tell you more when the sim is done."

"Well, I've still got my birds in the sky," Des noted. "I'm going to test their speed and estimate impact when they hit the wall. I've got one of these birds armed with my newest recipe."

"God, I hope you're not going to test the explosives right now too," Cy said as she exited the enclosed garden to the open glen so she could get a better look. "Allure, will you please stop him from blowing up our mountainside?"

"I'll try my best, but no guarantees," said Allure, while tracking Des's drones with a display on her VAGs. "Shit! Those things are moving fast. They're already up over 120 miles an hour!"

Just then, Des pulled back on the drones except for the one with the red paint on it. He continued flying that one at full speed, straight into a rock outcropping where it exploded on impact.

"Whoo!" shouted Michael.

When the dust settled, they saw that the explosives had cracked a car-sized granite boulder in two.

CHAPTER 15.

PHOENIX RISING

PRESENT DAY

Stonces is crumbled on the floor overwhelmed by grief. Damian kneels beside the sobbing and screaming Stonces in Adrianna's living room, and no amount of comfort Damian offers seems to calm him.

"I'm so sorry, my boy—so sorry," says Damian. "It … It was like what happened to your father. Someone hacked your mother's car and turned off power in a dangerous section. The car lost control and went off a cliff."

Stonces looks up at Damian, his dark skin blotchy and tear-streaked, and tries in vain to sniff the snot away. Damian hands him a silk handkerchief with his initials, D.S., stitched in gold on the edge. Stonces takes it gratefully and wipes his eyes and blows his nose.

"Where was my mother when she crashed? And what about her bodyguard?" Stonces asks as he chokes back more tears. "She … She told me she had extra security."

"I'm afraid it was my fault," Damian says, a little guilty. "She was driving home from meeting me in Paris, and the car crashed during the long drive back home. Her guard also died from blunt-force trauma."

Stonces has no idea that Damian, who's trying to act like a father to him now, is the man who really killed both of his parents in similar ways. But when Damian goes in for a hug, Stonces shrugs him off.

Even in the midst of this heartbreak, Stonces's wheels are already turning. Mother may be gone, but never forgotten. She just handed Stonces the keys to the GlobeCom kingdom, or what's left of it, as well as keys to the AI behind GlobeCom 2.0. He even has access to Damian's whole world, if he so chooses to explore it.

Stonces wisely keeps this information to himself.

Finally, he rises from the floor to stand and face the man he thinks of as an uncle. Instead of asking the obvious question, *Why would hackers kill my mom?* Stonces goes where his anger takes him, vowing to retaliate and protract this cyberwar.

"Just like with my dad seventeen years ago," he seethes. "I will find them and destroy them. They will *all* pay."

"Thataboy," Damian responds. "How can I help?"

As the elevator doors open to the Watergate employee lot, Saoirse bolts toward her father, a graying and fattening Skew, now fifty-two. She throws herself into his arms like the sixteen-year-old girl that she is and sobs hysterically.

"It was horrible. There was blood all over!" she cries.

Skew holds her tight, whispering comfort in his native tongue.

"It's OK. It's OK. Dar, you're safe now. Your da is here. You're safe," he says, petting her hair.

"Hate to interrupt, but I need Skew's help getting Mane into the chair," Allure breaks in. "It's going to take all four of us."

After Adam, Elven, Skew, and Allure perform a messy transfer to the wheelchair, Allure directs Adam to help her pull it up the ramp and into the van. Once in the small space of the van, they manage to secure the wheelchair and prop Mane's leg up on the leg rest with the help of some extra pillows tucked around it. Then Adam turns to go, but Allure catches him by the arm.

"Adam, can you stay back a minute?" she asks.

"What is it, Auntie? How can I help?"

"I know I've been hard on you, but this is real war, not the simulations in the workroom lab. You understand?" she says.

When he nods affirmative, she continues, "You did well today. You were very helpful, had great ideas, sacrificed R3x, and proved you are a man of valor, just like Des."

"Ah, Auntie, you embarrass me," Adam replies, his pale skin blushing a little. "I've been scared as shit this whole entire time. I'm still *petrified*."

"To my point! You overcome and do what needs to be done even in the face of sheer terror. Definition of valor," she affirms.

She inserts an IV into Mane's arm, and Adam tapes it down just like she'd taught him.

"It's time you know a few things ... before we part ways," Allure says.

"I don't want us to part. I ... We need you, especially now with Dad gone," he responds.

"And that's who I need to talk to you about," she answers soberly.

"Sounds ominous," Adam says, feeling worried.

"First, know that what I'm about to tell you was withheld from me until just yesterday morning," Allure explains. "Please don't judge them too harshly for not telling us."

"Yes, don't ask, don't tell, especially who someone is or was before they went off-grid. I get that," he says robotically.

"Exactly. But still, try to stay calm as I tell you," she says, pausing a moment. "Um ... Your mother was pregnant with you before she met Des ..."

"What?" Adam asks as the ramifications set in. "You mean, as in Des is *not* my father? That can't be true."

"Des loved you as if you were his blood," she starts to say before he interrupts her.

"Then ... then ... who?"

"Your biological father ... He's been financially supporting this operation the whole time," she answers. "Your father, biologically anyway, turns out to be none other than d_ArkAngl."

Adam looks shocked and then pissed.

"*Des is my father.* Not some rich guy financing us from afar. I don't care what you say," he explodes, pulling his hand from hers and trying to turn away. "I don't believe you. Why are you lying to me?"

"Look in the mirror, young Adam. That's why the Russians pointed their guns at you—because you look so damn much like him, like d_ArkAngl," Allure explains, using as much patience and gentleness as she can muster.

"But weren't the Russians after Leonard Smith?" Adam asks, putting two and two together. "So, are ... Are you saying d_ArkAngl and Leonard Smith are one and the same?"

"Yes, they are. But this must be kept between us," Allure acknowledges. "Leonard Smith is just too hot to be alive anymore. To throw the GlobeCom goons off our trail, we need everyone to think he's dead and that d_ArkAngl is a whole separate person."

"I can't accept that. No, I won't," Adam insists. "That arrogant bastard is *not* my father. Mom loves Des, who's nothing like that man out there."

They're interrupted by Saoirse calling to him from outside the van. "Adam? I need to talk to you," Saoirse says.

Adam looks at Allure. Unable to finish his thought, he throws his arms around her neck, and Allure holds him tight.

"I'm going to miss you, Auntie! You and Uncle Mane," he says emotionally. "I don't know where we're going, but Michael and I will find you again. Count on it."

"I believe you," Allure answers, patting his back. "Now get going. You don't have long to say goodbye."

Reluctantly, he pulls away from Allure and then hurries around the van and encounters Skew behind the wheel with Elven in the passenger seat next to him. d_ArkAngl is talking to Skew through the driver's side window as if they are newfound friends with Skew clasping d_ArkAngl's arm.

"And goodbye to you, Master Adam! Give your mom a big Skew-style hug for me when you meet up with her," he says as Adam passes by his window.

"Will do. Goodbye, Uncle Skew," Adam answers a little blankly.

Adam meets up with Saoirse who's watching the exit. He takes her hands in his and tries to speak. But her eyes carry a whole world—a universe of feelings, of lives yet to live, of new loss and fear of the unknown. Adam freezes there, in the world that is Saoirse's eyes, unable to talk.

"Um, I'm going to miss R3xie," says Saoirse, breaking the awkward silence. "He was the best robodog ever."

"It will be OK. R3x is having puppies, and R3x 2.0 will be even better. I saved his operating system and his apps," Adam says a little too quickly. "I'll be sure to make one for you."

"That would be nice to have a R3xie puppy," she says, stepping closer to him.

Adam looks down at his blood-splattered shoes, gathering his nerve. "I owe you a huge apology," he says before looking into her eyes again. "I ... I let my own insecurities get completely out of hand. I mean, I know you were never *with* him with him, and yet I was such an ass—to both of you."

"You *do* know that Michael is *gay*, right?" she asks. "He came out to me that night that you lost it, when you thought I was with *him*."

Adam looks confused.

"Really? Nothing? You never saw it? He likes boys instead of girls," she explains like a teacher would. "He had this huge crush on my brother Elven, and I told him that Elven, rightly, considers Michael jailbait and wouldn't touch him until he was at least eighteen."

Realization dawns on Adam's face. "Oh ... shit ... I really fucked up. I'm such a stupid jerk," Adam blurts. "But Michael's so butch. I mean, the muscle shirts and his manly good looks. But you're right. He follows Elven around like a puppy ... I was so stupid."

"Well, Michael said he was waiting for you to figure it out on your own. So, he was being an ass too," Saoirse confides.

"If he had just realized I'm thickheaded," Adam says regretfully. "I'm so sorry, so sorry."

Saoirse steps even closer, standing on her toes and wrapping her arms around his neck.

"The time lost between us all is what I'm most sorry for," she says sadly. "We lost a whole year. And now, when will we even see each other again?"

d_ArkAngl, who's near the exit stairs just outside of earshot, loudly clears his throat and speaks up. "OK, time to wrap it up and get on our way. There are still a few goons from GlobeCom about, and police will arrive any second," he reports.

Just then, they hear the sound of sirens approaching.

Adam takes Saoirse's face in both his hands. She leans in for their first kiss, sweet, lingering, and tender—a kiss that he'll remember for the rest of his life.

"Goodbye, little Saoirse," Adam says heavily as he lets her go. "Be safe."

Finally, Adam pulls away and walks dejectedly toward the waiting stranger who's supposedly his biological father.

TWELVE DAYS EARLIER

Cy, Des, Mane, and Allure left just after dark so they could meet up with the Cl0 clan and then make it to Oakridge by four in the morning.

Adam and Michael helped with logistics and packing, instructing the team where their items were in the Humvee, and demonstrating ways to avoid being scanned by cameras and drones.

After team backbone left, the UFJ compound felt eerily quiet. Except for Wizard and R3x, Michael and Adam were alone on the vast, ten-thousand-acre property. That's not to say that they weren't busy. For the first time, they got to hack out in the wild by knocking on GlobeCom's cyberdoors and preparing entry for team backbone.

Their primary mission was to pave the way by parking malicious scripts at the emergency response system access points, waiting for the emergency response network to come alive. The emergency response network was GlobeCom's Achilles' heel. Because the network only turns on when an emergency is underway, it wasn't monitored like the rest of GlobeCom.

At three o'clock in the morning, Michael and Adam were at the controls in the workroom when they heard R3x bark upstairs, followed by Wizard authenticating.

"Hi, boys," Wizard said as he entered the workroom. "We got another message from d_ArkAngl."

"What'd it say?" asked Michael, still watching his screen to make sure they'd left no trace of evidence that could lead investigators back to this location.

"Bilbo is definitely in Work Camp 74," Wizard answered.

"Isn't the new GlobeCom AI build coming out of Work Camp 74?" Michael asked. "I think we've got some data on that camp somewhere."

"Well, that's great news, isn't it?" Adam exclaimed. "We can get him out now."

"I'm afraid d_ArkAngl can't do anything from the inside at this moment with Operation Backbone already in play," Wizard responded. "And he's not sure he can trust Bilbo. He thinks Bilbo's been indoctrinated and is leading the new AI development."

CHAPTER 16.

BRAVE NEW WORLD

PRESENT DAY

Adam watches forlornly as the van carrying Saoirse follows the service exit up to the next level.

"I know what you're going through, Son, and I'm sorry, but we have to leave now," says d_ArkAngl who's still waiting by the stairs.

"You couldn't possibly know what I'm going through, and I'm not your son. I'm Des's son," says Adam as he reluctantly crosses the garage to the stairwell.

He may be a bit self-absorbed, but d_ArkAngl isn't heartless. Every time he had to leave Cy behind, he felt what Adam must be feeling now. Hiding himself away from Adam was even worse than leaving Cy behind. So, naturally, Adam's words and anger cut him to the core. But he says nothing because this isn't about him. It's about a seventeen-year-old who's seen and lost so much in such a short time.

When they emerge at street level, response vehicles race past them and down Virginia Avenue toward the main hotel entrance. The two of them act as cool as cucumbers, nothing out of the ordinary, just two travelers looking for transport, although, in reality, their senses are on high alert. They cross over a drive-through between the C-shaped Watergate Hotel and the J-shaped Watergate office building. Their destination is at the bottom end of the J shape past the post office and the rented business suites.

They step through automatic glass doors that say "Atlantic Travel and Limousine," and d_ArkAngl instructs Adam to hide his face from the cameras.

"Keep your eyes down so the scanners can't pick up your attributes," he advises. "Not that anyone has any files on you, but you don't want to start one either."

Although GlobeCom central is down, local cameras are still taking images and storing them in their local drives. So, Adam follows d_ArkAngl's lead as he registers for their car at the self-serve kiosk.

"This is where I rent my cars when I see your mother. I know their systems, and I can easily tap into their tracking apps to hide my activities," he explains. "The rental agency thinks I'm some-one else and turns a blind eye to any log anomalies, mostly because of the generous tips I leave in the vehicle's payment vault."

Five minutes later, the two of them buckle up in a self-driving futuristic-looking Jeep All Terrain (JAT) and pull right onto Virginia Avenue. As they do, Adam examines their rental car.

"I've seen these! This is a top-of-the-line solar model for on- and off-road. It can even go amphibian if required," Adam says a little too excitedly. "One of my favorite vehicles."

"Mine too," d_ArkAngl agrees.

He issues a command to his wrist controller, "Initiate

geolocation masking program." To Adam, he explains, "You can never be too careful with the logs."

"How does it work?" Adam asks, curious. "And how is the car self-driving with satellites down?"

"Most of the cars you see on the road right now are self-driving, actually," d_ArkAngl notes. "Once the GlobeCom backbone went down, the vehicle systems reset to operate on proximity sensors using the latest routes stored in local memory."

"Oh, makes sense," says Adam as he starts tinkering with the console. "Do you like silver?"

"Sounds as good a color as any," d_ArkAngl answers.

"Well if you like silver, then I'm picking another color," Adam retorts.

He turns the car a glossy luminescent black.

d_ArkAngl shrugs, amused at Adam's little rebellion.

"It's normally a thirty-five-minute drive to the Potomac Airfield from here, but we'll be using the back roads, so it will take us almost an hour. And when we get there, the airfield will be a little rough. It's been out of service for twenty years, give or take."

Adam says nothing as he looks out the window, tuning out the stranger next to him who's trying to be his father.

After a while, d_ArkAngl tries again. "Bossa told me you just lost Des in the firefight outside of Oakridge," he says delicately. "I feel sick over the news. I know he was like a father to you."

"He was the *only* father to me," Adam answers bitterly.

"I'd hoped Des would come to love you and your mother like I do. And that he'd be a real father to you, and I see he was," d_ArkAngl agrees, trying to diffuse him.

Adam goes quiet again as they cross the Eleventh Street Bridge and blend into the Barry Farm District.

"I'm here if you want to talk or have questions," he continues. "This must be so confusing—"

"Don't ask, don't tell," Adam says bitterly, shutting d_ArkAngl down.

Not wanting to push any further, he allows Adam his space as they continue in silence for another ten minutes.

"So, my first question," Adam finally says. "What's the nature of your relationship with my mother?"

"That's a very good question. Your mother and I go way back. We met before she went off-grid. We knew each other closely and intimately," d_ArkAngl explains. "She was and is most precious to me—besides you, of course."

"Yeah, me, who you abandoned in the woods so many years ago, along with your other most precious thing—Mom," Adam accuses.

"It wasn't like that. I was there right after your birth with you and your mother, like a real family. We bonded. I held you for hours. I *named* you ... But coming to see you, with GlobeCom monitoring my every move? That would put all of you—and me—at great risk. It was for everyone's safety that I had to stay away."

Adam rolls his eyes in disagreement and looks out the window at the darkening evening sky.

"OK, second question. Why not join us off the grid?" Adam asks.

"Well, I was under the thumb of two superpowers, both of whom wouldn't just let me go my merry way. And then there were the resources," d_ArkAngl says, looking into Adam's eyes. "I needed to stay behind to support you and the clans financially and logistically as the resistance grew."

d_ArkAngl senses that Adam is walking a fine line trying to hold it together.

"It's been hard for all of us," he continues as gently as he can. "And I'm most sorry about the pain this is causing you now, on top of everything else you've just been through."

Adam somehow manages not to cry, shout, or throw himself out of the car, although he wants to do all three at once. Instead, he smolders quietly in the seat beside this stranger who is now his father. Meanwhile, the one who raised him is six feet under at Des0l8tion Ridge.

When they reach the end of Rose Valley Drive, d_ArkAngl sets the car to camouflage mode. The Jeep drives silently and blends into the night, going unnoticed as it passes the few homes along the drive.

"Hold on. We're going off-road," he says to Adam. Then, to the car, he adds, "Manual mode override."

"Manual not permittable," the car responds in a female voice.

"Override authorization 1762255xyb," d_ArkAngl says back to the car as it comes to the end of road.

The car slows and jerks as he gains control of steering and acceleration. He drives slowly around the barricade at the end of the paved road and onto a dirt road leading to the old, abandoned airstrip.

As the Jeep bounces over pits and mounds of the decaying landing strip, a small plane swoops overhead, lights off, so quiet that it sounds like a whisper in the wind. After a bumpy landing, it lurches to a stop at the far end of the abandoned landing strip. d_ArkAngl drives up to the plane and parks the car. Then he hands Adam a remote control.

"Please steer this car back to the finished part of the road," he instructs. "Once it hits the hard road surface with named streets, autopilot will kick back on and point it toward its home base."

"All while overwriting the log data on the way home too?" Adam asks.

"That's right. And there's another huge tip in the pay pocket so that they won't care about discrepancies," d_ArkAngl answers as he takes his case and steps out of the car.

"Where are you going?" Adam asks.

"I'll be on the plane. Bossa and I have some catching up to do."

d_ArkAngl strides quickly and confidently toward Bossa's homemade six-man plane.

"So ... fucking ... mysterious," Adam says sarcastically under his breath as the man walks away.

A few minutes later, Adam steps onto the marked gangway and then into the cockpit where he immediately notices the musty scent of livestock.

"God it smells like a barn in here," Adam complains as he settles into the seat behind d_ArkAngl.

"Ask your mom about that," Bossa suggests. "Your family insisted on bringing all your chickens and your goat when I collected them at the dinky Ingalls Airport out on a narrow ridgetop yesterday."

Once buckled in, Adam gets his first real look at the mysterious Bossa. She's nearly seventy, petite, and pear-shaped with long gray hair and a lifetime of wrinkles. She looks more like an apple doll than the international British spy Adam thought she'd be.

"*This* is Bossa?" Adam asks, surprised.

Bossa turns from her controls and closely inspects him with her small, steely eyes. "Got a problem with that?" asks Bossa who speaks with a gritty voice.

"Um, no, ma'am," Adam responds, taken aback.

"Don't mess with me, kid. You don't know who you're dealing with," Bossa continues. "I've moved the rest of your family and your livestock to California, and now I'm here to retrieve your sorry asses because, like always, your father is late to the party."

"Ah, Bossa. I see your demeanor hasn't changed over the years," d_ArkAngl says affectionately.

"Well ... You've changed," Bossa responds. "You're a father, so I'm told ... nearly eighteen years after the fact."

"I'd tell you if you needed to know. So now, you need to know," he parlays back.

"Such a smart-ass! That much hasn't changed," Bossa responds.

"Wait! Weren't your eyes brown a minute ago?" Adam asks d_ArkAngl.

"Yes, kid, that's on me because your dad's brown contact lenses were creeping me out, and I asked him to remove them," Bossa answers. "Nobody's recording him in this bird—or where we'll be going, so you might as well get comfortable and be yourselves."

"So how are Mom and Michael?" Adam asks, changing subjects. "Do they like where we are going?"

"Your mother was kind of in shock, so hard to tell ... But I've never seen a stronger woman who's suddenly strapped to a wheelchair after losing a husband to boot," Bossa says thoughtfully.

"Cy is in a wheelchair?! What the hell?" d_ArkAngl bursts. "Nobody told me Cy was hurt. Allure said she is safe."

"Oh, sorry. No time to tell you during all the shooting and the blood and stuff," says Adam a little sarcastically.

"What's this about shootings and blood?" Bossa asks.

Adam and d_ArkAngl start talking at once, telling her the highlights as she double-checks her gauges for takeoff.

Bossa stops them, growing concerned. "Is anyone following you?" she asks.

"We don't think so," Adam answers.

His father looks around to be sure.

"Well I'm not taking any chances. We've got to move now. Prepare for takeoff," Bossa says. "Headsets on, seatbelts buckled. And hang on. Despite how smooth I made the landing look, it wasn't easy. It'll be even harder taking off."

As she prepares her instruments, Adam watches with rapt attention.

"These instruments aren't digital ... They're analog, aren't they?" he observes. "So *old school.*"

"That's right, kid. The compass is a real magnetic sensor.

And I'm fond of push controls because they don't emit any signals that can get us discovered along our route," she explains. "Got a problem with that?"

"No. No problem. I think it's cool," he agrees. "It also looks as if you built this plane yourself. I can't even tell what model it is."

"Well, yes, with a little help from an old plane kit and a few parts I had lying around," she says, starting to warm up to him.

"Impressive," Adam replies, meaning it.

She flips on night vision and then taxies the plane for takeoff. "This plane has a fully charged Tesla battery. We will make it cross-country without stopping," she says as the plane speeds up down the bumpy runway. "We should be landing in about seven hours. But be aware: We're on our own out here. No flight plan, no control towers, nobody to know but us if our flight goes down somewhere."

"Oh, that's reassuring," Adam responds. "And didn't Tesla go out of business about eight years ago?"

"Yes. But their solar storage is still the bomb," Bossa says. "By the way, are you hungry?"

Both men's stomachs rumble at the mention of food.

"Actually, yes, I guess I am," Adam answers.

"Great. Now it's like I have two kids to feed!" she says, giving them both a hard time. "You're lucky I've got you covered. And you can thank your mother for that. She sent the cooler beside you there, Adam."

Adam opens the cooler strapped to the seat next to him to find sandwiches and drinks.

"I'll take the ham on rye please. And one of those Yerba Mates that she makes. I need the caffeine ... But first use the wipes to clean up," she instructs.

"Um, they're all ham on rye," Adam says as he looks through the cooler.

"Well, beggars can't be choosers," she responds.

Adam pulls some clean wipes for himself and passes them forward to Bossa. Then he begins the slow process of cleaning the dried blood from his fingernails and the cracks of his knuckles.

"You're lucky we have food," Bossa continues testily. "Food, my dear, is getting hard to come by with GlobeCom down."

"Local distribution systems are already emerging throughout the world," d_ArkAngl responds. "The global distribution system will take much longer to rebuild."

Adam is almost too upset to eat by the time he finally cleans his knuckles and nails of Mane's blood. Then his stomach growls again, and he manages to wolf down two sandwiches and a bottle of water.

Shortly after, as the plane hums onward at 34,000 feet, Adam's eyelids become heavy. His head nods and bobs as he dozes in and out. A collage of images flashes through his mind's eye: Goons coming at them with weapons drawn. Mane covered in blood. R3x firing. Saoirse's tender kiss goodbye …

Finally, he falls into a fitful sleep.

For a while, the two adults are silent as they eat their sandwiches and take in the horizon.

"The kid looks just like you, by the way," Bossa says once she's done with her dinner. "He's smart and even a little entitled like you, but he also has a healthy streak of insecurity—something I've never detected in you before. How's he holding up?"

d_ArkAngl sets his sandwich down and starts ticking off events.

"Well, there were a lot of firsts for him," he notes. "First, the only father Adam's ever known died in Operation Backbone, while his mother was left crippled during the same operation. His godfather was gravely wounded in front of him just four hours ago. He directed drones and robots for the first time in deadly warfare where bad guys got sliced to bits. Then he finds out his father is not his biological father but that I am—and he doesn't seem to like me much. Now he's leaving the only home he's known."

He pauses a second, thinking. "Did I forget anything? Oh yeah, he had to leave his pretty girlfriend behind. And I overheard her telling Adam that his brother is gay—something Adam seemed to know nothing about until today."

Bossa takes her eyes off the horizon long enough to look back at Adam sleeping like an angel. "All in all, I'd say we're lucky he's not screaming like a lunatic back there," she surmises.

"Mane had better pull through because Adam and Michael don't need to deal with another loss," d_ArkAngl adds.

"Met Michael on the flight over," Bossa notes. "A delightful young man, albeit protective of Cy. He's like her own secret service detail. I take it he gets that from Des."

d_ArkAngl nods affirmatively. "Well it didn't come from me," he says, leaning back in his seat. "By the way, do you have any Dom?"

"You're still a spoilt rich kid just like when I met you," she admonishes. "Nope. No champagne on this flight. I need you to stay awake and keep me on my toes."

"Fine," he says, reaching for another Yerba Matte.

"We're headed to the north coast where I bought an entire canyon for a song," she informs him. "It's in an area that used to be called Monte Rio on the Russian River, which is running again. Trees are growing back, and we've stabilized the landslide areas. We're using horses and pack mules and the occasional golf cart to get around. And there's a private cabin for you and Cy to share, which she seems agreeable to."

"How is Cy feeling? How is she doing with all these changes?" he asks.

"Like I said, never a stronger woman," Bossa answers. "I think overall she is still in top form despite the damage to her spine."

"Is everything set up for her to rehab at the camp?" he asks.

"Not sure. We don't have a clan doctor where we're going. Wizard's in charge of following up on Cy's therapy, and he's pretty creative," she says with a smile of appreciation. "He's already using my hitching posts as arm supports while she learns to walk again."

"So, there's hope for her to live a normal life?" he asks.

"Define *normal* … because none of us live *normal* lives," Bossa responds. "But if you're asking, 'Will she walk again?' I think she will. Here's a question to you, though: Does it matter?"

Taken aback, he replies, "Not to *me*. We've had too much time apart for me to care about things like that. But if I know Cy, she won't be happy until she's running and gardening again. So, for her sake, I think it really does matter."

"Good answer, boy. We raised you right after all," Bossa says approvingly.

"So, you and Wiz … Were you happy to see Wizard again?" he asks. "Are you sharing a cabin? Are you two a thing again?"

"A lady never tells," Bossa responds, flashing a wicked smile.

The conversation pauses while Bossa checks her flight path. They are approaching the central plains, and turbulence begins bumping the small plane around like a toy.

"Make sure Adam's buckled in tight. I'm ascending to 38,000 feet where we'll miss the worst of it, but it is going to get rougher," Bossa instructs.

When d_ArkAngl doesn't answer, she turns to see him sound asleep, despite the turbulence. Bossa looks at him with loving disapproval.

"Some copilot *you* are," she admonishes.

Five hours later, the men are rudely awakened by Bossa's cursing as she maneuvers the plane eastward to get out of a busy airport flight path.

"Who'd have thought there'd be so many planes in the air

without the central systems working?" she's saying mostly to herself. "We're too close to Oakland and SFO, and their damn control towers are pinging me on the radio for my call sign."

Instead of answering the towers, Bossa diverts the plane east to peel away toward Modesto.

Adam needs to pee badly but doesn't want to use his container, so he tries to hold it.

"Um. How long till we land?" he asks. "And where are we going to land, exactly?"

"We're landing in about fifteen minutes on what used to be the Healdsburg Municipal Airport," she answers.

"Wait! Didn't that whole area burn down—like four or five times?" Adam asks. "I heard north of San Francisco is an abandoned wasteland."

"You heard right, kid. I see you're keeping abreast of history," Bossa responds. "Yes, burned and abandoned. The fires and droughts and all that business with the power company never getting its shit together pretty much sealed it. All the while, the price of water grew out of reach for most home and business owners."

"Right, I read about the rolling blackouts in the summertime when drought was at its worst and people needed electricity most. Fires broke out in 2017 and 2018, the lightning storms and fire tornadoes of 2020, the first year of the pandemic, followed by major fires every summer thereafter until finally everyone from the area moved away," Adam recalls.

Just then, the sun rises over the eastern horizon, turning the sky into a kaleidoscope of color. They fly straight into the blinding sun until they reach what used to be the town of Napa. Then she lowers her altitude to twenty thousand feet and banks north again over what used to be the river town of Petaluma.

The land below looks like a war zone, a patchwork of burned-out desolation, tumbleweeds, and new growth springing up in the cracks and then withering under the sun. The Petaluma River, once a main waterway that connected the town to Napa and Marin counties, is dry.

Then they pass over what used to be Santa Rosa, with miles of burnt foundations and blackened swimming pools. A few uninhabited buildings are amazingly intact, such as the old Charles Schultz ice arena that is still standing, untouched, with nothing around it but burned-out rubble.

As they pass north of Santa Rosa, Bossa begins the full descent. This is where they cross over the only green in the land. Stubby trees and weedy shrubs grow along both edges of the Russian River that snakes slowly west to the coast. The river is more a creek than the majestic river it used to be, and the muddy waterway is strewn with burnt organic matter. Still, it is beautiful as the gray waters flash like hematite in the morning sun.

"The Healdsburg Dam and fish gate are gone, along with the old walking bridge above it," Bossa says, reminiscing.

As they fly over the town square, all that's left are sidewalks that slice through what used to be a park with a round cement foundation in the park's center.

"There was a gazebo in the middle there," Bossa continues. "To think I used to sip my J brut and my Rodney Strong red blends to live music out in that plaza under the shade of hundred-year-old trees."

They approach the old airport, now devoid of buildings save for a pile of rubble where the landing tower used to be. Adam looks out the window to the runway with alarm.

"Can we even land there?" he asks.

"It's going to be tight, only twenty-five hundred feet, not all of it functional, usually need three thousand feet," Bossa says. "Already did it once, so should be OK. I think."

"That doesn't make me fell at all warm and fuzzy," Adam says, checking his seat belt and wishing he didn't have to pee so badly.

"Don't worry, kid. I've got this. Ask your dad about me and airplanes," Bossa responds.

d_ArkAngl, clinging to his armrest just a little too tightly for Adam's liking, tries to reassure him. "Um, that's right. Bossa's been the star of many airshows back in the day. And a flight instructor," he says, trying to sound convincing. "If anyone can land on a dime, it's Bossa."

As their plane approaches, they see three figures waiting for them at end of the runway. d_ArkAngl recognizes Cy immediately, and his breath catches in his chest.

Instead of looking broken like he expected, Cy sits straight and regal in her chair, supported from a back brace. Michael stands on one side of her, Wizard on the other, each with a hand resting respectfully on her shoulders.

Cy, aglow in the morning light, looks out at the plane expectantly as it touches down and comes to a safe but jerky stop.

End of Book 1

Watch for two more books in the *Breaking Backbones* Hacker Trilogy:

- **Book II:** *Information Should Be Free*
- **Book III:** *Out of Chaos Comes Order*

ACKNOWLEDGEMENTS

My sincere thanks to the many experts and friends who reviewed different drafts of this book for accuracy and readability, starting with my friends and coworkers who I left behind at the SANS Institute, Suzanne Schleisman and Jill DeRosa. They encouraged me after reading the first version I sent them (which was pretty rough), and even tried to sell the story concept to old publishing contacts of theirs. I'd like to thank my nephew Bobby and niece Sierra, who gave the book the non-technical 'young people' read and encouraged me to slow it down a little! And thanks to Ian Poynter for an early review to confirm technical accuracy, which I needed before I could go any further with editing. Thanks, also, to Tyler L. Jones for a followup read of the more finished draft and who loved the characters and approved the technical depictions within the story, ultimately encouraging me to go on with the publishing process. And to cyberthreat intel hobbiest Jonathan Lark, thanks for providing relevant tech details to fill in the story. Finally, and most importantly, I want to thank my mom, a fellow writer who listened to my story over the phone and helped me develop some of the characters, particularly the bad guy characters like Damian Strand.

It takes a community to fight cybercrime and I've been fortunate to be considered part of that community since the mid-1990's even though I come from a journalist background rather than from the technology side.

Some of the characters (Colonel Chris James at DoD forensics lab, Mane, Allure, Bilbo, d_ArkAngl, Gabriel Dupres and Bossa) are composites of real people I've met during my twenty-five-year career as an investigative journalist in cybercrime and cybersecurity and they've approved this message. Thanks to all of you and so many more characters that I couldn't fit into this story. *Without your shared knowledge, the cybercriminals would be light years ahead of the cyberdefenders.*